RENOVATING HIS HEART

STELLA GRACE

BLUSHING BOOKS

Published by Blushing Books®,
a subsidiary of
ABCD Graphics and Design
977 Seminole Trail #233
Charlottesville, VA 22901
The trademark Blushing Books®
is registered in the US Patent and Trademark Office.

Stella Grace
Renovating His Heart

EBook ISBN: 978-1-61258-794-3
Print ISBN:978-1-61258-695-3
Cover Art by ABCD Graphics & Design

MEET AND GREET

$\mathcal{T}$y Parks spread out his construction plans on the hood of his sleek new black truck. Something wasn't right. He looked at the forms on the ground, then back at the plans, his brown eyes scanning for a discrepancy. Pounding his fist on the truck, Ty confirmed the subcontractor had laid out the forms for the concrete sidewalk on the wrong side of the site.

"Dammit all." Another day lost because of his incompetent subs. He reached for his phone on his hip, anger rushing through his veins. Ty really didn't want his Monday to start off this way.

"John, it's Ty Parks with Evans' Construction. We've got a problem."

Twenty minutes later, a mixture of Ty's workers and the chastised subcontractor, along with his crew, arrived at the site, coffee cups in hand, bragging about their eventful weekends.

Ty barked, and everyone scattered to their various assignments around the site.

That was the usual routine for Ty. Arrive early, find an

issue, bark until it got fixed, go home, and repeat the next day. He never got to be the nice guy, and he never got a break. It must have been part of his job description, buried really deep in the small print.

James Guiser, his top laborer, approached him with an inquisitive face, pushing his overgrown blond hair out of his face. James was twenty-three-years-old, going on seventeen, and had the party attitude of a college student, though he had never stepped foot on a campus.

Ty appreciated the younger man's zest to party from time to time, especially the couple of months following his breakup with his old girlfriend, Stephanie.

"You don't want to know," Ty responded to James' questioning expression and stepped away from him to observe one of the framers as he placed a 2x4. When James continued to look at him with raised eyebrows, Ty enlightened him quietly. "The concrete guys put the forms in the wrong spot." He nodded at the man working frantically to move the forms.

"No, shit. Really?" James threw his arms up, mocking Ty's frustration. Ty rolled his eyes.

"Now we have to wait until they finish so we can pour the concrete," he told James and anyone else who was in earshot, including the berated subcontractor.

As much as he regretted it, Ty also knew he had to call his boss. Mr. Evans needed to know there was a delay. Again.

He excused himself from James and turned to make the call, walking toward the far end of the construction site where it wasn't as noisy.

Bill Evans was a hard man to work for and an even harder man to impress. He expected professionalism, punctuality, and a good work ethic from all of his employees. He didn't tolerate laziness and incompetence; neither did he have patience for delays.

Ty had started at Evans' Construction as a simple laborer,

just like James, at the age of twenty-three. Nine years later, he ran his own jobs as the highest paid employee of the company. Mr. Evans also had pride in Ty and respected how hard he'd worked to gain his approval. He just recently hinted that he would like Ty to take the company in the event that his deteriorating health finally took his life.

Mr. Evans had been diagnosed with liver cancer several months ago. He had refused chemotherapy and was making arrangements to ensure his family and company would survive long after his passing. One of those arrangements was giving the family business to Ty in exchange for twenty-five percent of the profits toward his estate.

"Jason, help Quinn move those boards. Let's get this moved so we can be ready when the concrete arrives at ten." Ty spewed out more orders after getting off the phone with Mr. Evans. His men, as expected, obeyed and shifted into action. There were never issues about resisting Ty's orders, and no one tried to overstep and go against Ty's authority. He knew how to run a job, and he was respected for it.

The sound of gravel crackling below the weight of tires came up behind him, but Ty didn't turn around. He was too focused on the activity flaming in front of him.

Bright headlights dimmed as the sound of the quiet engine cut off while Ty crossed his well-defined arms over his chest and studied the activity in front of him.

He finally turned around just as a twenty-nine-year-old woman placed her shapely legs out of the candy-apple red sports car. She wore vivid red stiletto heels, which hugged her petite feet perfectly. Ty took a moment to ogle the beautiful woman as she stood with her long legs gracefully taking on the weight of her fit body. She wore dressy black shorts and a business casual top accented by costume jewelry.

Noticing the calm that blanketed the site, Ty turned to find most of his men had stopped to look at the mysterious woman as well.

He cleared this throat. They didn't have time to waste gawking at the magnificent creature who clearly didn't belong on his construction site.

"Excuse me! We only have a couple of hours before the concrete arrives. Let's go!" he yelled, and his men quickly swarmed back to work.

Once he was satisfied that the distraction was no longer an issue, Ty turned his attention back to the beauty approaching him with a box of donuts in her hand.

She had long, smooth, chocolate colored hair hanging down her back, which looked recently trimmed and styled. She didn't appear to be wearing any makeup and clearly didn't need to.

"Are you Ty?" her singsong voice asked him.

"Yes. Can I help you?" He regretted how blunt his words sounded but, in his defense, it was not a good time.

"Ty, I'm Grace. I'm here to help you manage this job," she collectedly told him, extending her delicate hand while balancing the donuts in the other.

Ty couldn't hold back the howl of laughter that rose from his gut. He didn't accept her handshake and flashed a bright smile.

"Oh, sweetheart, that's a good one. Who sent you? Bill?" Ty asked her with laughter remaining in his eyes.

She didn't waver, humor absent from her sky-blue eyes.

"If you mean Bill Evans, then, yes, he sent me."

"You can tell Bill I said thank you for the laugh and the donuts," he responded, appraising her body with his hungry eyes. He reached out and graciously took the donuts from her with a coy smile on his lips.

"I'm sorry. I think you misunderstand why I'm here, Mr. Parks. I'm not here for your visual pleasure. I'm here to help manage," she said and tilted her chin just a little higher.

Her tone sobered Ty just a little.

"I'm sorry. I don't need help," he told her, switching gears and flashing her a coy smile.

"Mr. Evans advised me there was an issue with a subcontractor this morning?" Now, her eyes held a hint of amusement, which clouded them like a slate blue storm.

"There was, but as you can see it's been handled, and we are back on schedule," he smiled, trying his hardest to hide the discontent flowing in his veins.

She raised her voice so that everyone on the site could hear her, "Maybe I should introduce myself and get started on the right foot."

Ty tried to keep his anger in check and shifted uncomfortably on his feet. Maybe this was a test to see if he would get distracted.

"So, Mr. Parks, I would like to formally introduce myself. I'm Grace Evans, Bill Evans' daughter." She extended her manicured hand firmly out again.

This time, Ty accepted it as his jaw dropped wide open.

LESSON

*G*race apprehensively stepped out of her car, anxiety flooding her veins as the all-male construction crew assessed her looks. She had spent hours that morning in front of the mirror debating the best outfit for her big debut. She refused to reduce herself to jeans and a polo shirt just because that's what the industry deemed appropriate.

Grace wanted to make a statement, damn it, and red stilettos made a statement. However, as Ty Parks slowly undressed her with his eyes, Grace regretted her overly feminine outfit. She wished she hadn't gone against the norm, just this once.

She tried to speak with confidence and knowledge because her father warned her that men in construction were just that: men in construction. It wasn't a world where women excelled. Testosterone levels thrived on job sites, and there was a sense of masculinity that she knew she would feel the moment her shoes hit the ground. Construction workers were usually hard men who built big muscles. It was a stereotype older than the country she lived in.

But Grace was determined to prove them all wrong. A

woman could do a man's job. She was strong, with impressive muscles. She didn't have a body building physique, but she wasn't a delicate lady either.

"Why do you want to go into construction? It's a man's field," her college boyfriend, Ben, had challenged her many times as they lay in bed contemplating their lives.

"Because Evans' Construction has been passed down for generations, and I don't want the family business to end just because my dad had a girl," she always answered.

And that was the truth. Any time discussions about the business had come up, her father always had the same answer: "No. A woman has no place in construction."

So, Grace paid her own way through college, even after her father cut off her funding, working a night job while she finished her studies. She graduated with a degree in construction management and diligently pursued a job at some of the top-ranking general contractors in the area.

Reality hit her and burst her bubble when rejection letters came in the mail. It didn't matter that she was at the top of her class or that her father was in construction. She knew all of the rejections were due to her gender.

Now, as she stood in front of Ty Parks in, what she considered appropriate shorts and clean hair, Grace regretted spending the latter part of her life in school for this. She wavered in her resolve for a short moment, wondering if she had made a mistake in asking her father for an internship. For the first time, she was feeling the rock-hard wall of rejection.

But Grace wouldn't let Ty bring her down. She tipped her head high and spoke with confidence.

"I would like to formally introduce myself. I'm Grace Evans, Bill Evans' daughter," she stated, extending her hand out again.

Boy, did his jaw drop. It felt amazing.

Grace paused for a moment when his rather large hand encased hers. He was all man. There was no doubt about that.

7

The rugged callus on his palm told her that much. One small glance at the taut, powerful muscles on his arms showed her he was a strong construction worker who knew how to get dirty and work hard.

She pulled her dainty but capable hand away and continued to smile her winning smile even though it felt like a dog was thrashing apart her insides.

"Ms. Evans, I'm sorry. I had no clue," he told her with a reserved smile. His tone didn't waver, and he didn't cower. Ty just accepted his mistake and took ownership as a real man would.

Real man, now, that was a new concept. She had had limited experience with boys. Those in high school were too young and immature to call men and her one and only college boyfriend, Ben, didn't want to be with a woman who was willing to cross gender lines and take a career in construction. It seemed to go against his moral compass.

"Apology accepted. Now that we have that out of the way, my dad informed me you might need help with a pour this morning."

"Nope. Everything's under control," Ty said. He rolled up the sleeves of his green shirt, which distracted Grace for a second time. The muscles in his arms were well-defined and tan.

"I see that, but what about the grades? Has the soil been tested over there?" She continued as she swallowed the frog climbing up her throat.

Ty paused to look at her, amazement in his eyes. She displayed a smile over the small victory.

"Yes, the soil was tested. The damn sub just laid it out in the wrong spot over the weekend."

"Oh, was no one here to supervise?" she jested with a sweet voice. Hell, he deserved it after his rude introduction.

"No," he said. "We've used this sub for years. I trust them. We've never had a problem until now."

Grace could feel the annoyance dripping from his words.

"Okay. Makes sense. As long as it's resolved." She smiled, taking a few more strategic steps onto the job site. Thank God, her heels weren't sinking into the dirt.

"How long do you plan on staying because I really don't need someone to supervise me?" he asked as he ran a hand through his short dark hair. The gesture drew her attention away from the site and back to his highly attractive appearance. He was clearly frustrated with her presence.

"I'm just going to the different job sites today. I won't stay long. I promise." She kept her tone even and crisp.

"Good," Ty muttered under his breath before answering the phone buzzing on his hip. He turned away from her as he spoke, which allowed her a moment to study him.

Ty was a bigger man than she had expected. Her father spoke about him a lot but never discussed his looks or age. Grace had always pictured a plump man with a round face in his mid-forties. Instead, Ty had expansive, well-sculptured shoulders supported by a very cut waist. He clearly didn't favor Chinese and donuts, like she had imagined. He was a lot younger than she thought too, maybe a couple of years older than her twenty-nine. Images of sexy construction workers with chiseled abs came to mind.

This was Ty Parks, the man her father chose to give his company to.

He combed his well-worked hands through his hair again, a gesture she had begun to understand as frustration, obviously about something the other person was expressing. He yelled into his phone, "I don't fucking have time for this. He needs to be here, *now*!"

She realized his height when he ducked to avoid a branch as he paced the site during his phone call. He was much taller than her short five-foot-five. She studied his stance as he paced, his arms animating his conversation. He was miffed but accepting whatever he was being told.

He returned to Grace after placing his phone back into the holster on his belt which hung low on his hips.

"Your dad says you're to remain here the rest of the day," Ty explained to her, the words coming in an exhale.

"You were just using that profane language toward my father?" She couldn't hide the shock in her voice.

"Hell, no! I'm not that stupid. One of our laborers just called in. He's hungover."

"So, I assume that's why I'm staying here?"

"Yup. I hope you brought a pair of work boots because we're going to get dirty," he said, amusement in his voice.

He looked up and down her bare legs, publicly appraising her. The humor in his eyes indicated that he expected her to squirm.

Little did he know, she always came prepared.

SHOCK THERAPY

*T*y watched her, waiting for the unease to settle in. If she wanted to prove herself, then she needed to get her hands dirty, and Ty was willing to hand her the shovel.

She paused for just a moment, the debate over her next move painted on her face. Her eyes, blue like an oasis pool, shone with apprehension. Ty expected her to cower and leave. Instead, much to his surprise, Grace stood taller.

"I'll be right back," she announced, turning on her petite heel and heading back to her dinky car. He stared when she bent over into the back seat to collect something. Her legs were amazingly sculpted, tan, and tight. The shorts were a little too long to see the crease where her bottom met her legs, but his imagination filled in the gap. When she stood up, she produced a pair of ripped jeans and new construction boots.

"Any place I can change?" she asked, holding her jeans high in her hands.

Ty paused for a moment, then said, "Not really." She needed to learn the hard way, even if her lesson was making him hard.

"Okay." She looked around, clearly surveying her options.

"My car's too small to jump into my jeans. I'll just go right over there behind that tree. Just make sure no one's looking," she told him as she walked toward the scant tree behind him.

"Are you kidding?" By the time the concrete arrived, every man on site would have to 'use the restroom'.

"Do you have a better idea?"

God, she was making him hard. *What the hell?* He'd turned away from strong women when his ex proved they were too much work.

"The porta-john's right over there," he told her, pointing in the far corner of the lot. He couldn't have her undressing in public. Lord knew the kind of things that would get back to his boss.

"Oh, great. I didn't see it." She smiled and bounced her way toward it, seemingly unaffected.

"I figured you didn't see it," he mumbled sarcastically under his breath. Then, with her out of sight, he refocused his distracted men.

"Come on, let's go. You've got an hour!" he yelled and slapped his hands together.

"Sorry, Ty, it's hard to concentrate." One of his workers smirked as he nodded toward the porta-john.

"Well, get used to it. She's going to be around for a while," he lectured them and himself.

Damn.

Ty's phone rang again, and he turned to answer it just as she was returning. The jeans were an improvement, but she was still not construction laborer material.

"This is Ty," he answered, holding his finger up at her. He wasn't going to change how he did things just because his boss' daughter wanted to prove herself. He continued his conversation then hung up the phone. She spoke before he could.

"Where should I get started?"

"Concrete's on its way," he announced to everyone. Then he

focused on her, "You need to help the guys level the ground over there," he told her and handed her a leveling rake.

To his surprise, she jumped right in with the guys, not complaining once as she worked with them to get the ground ready. Ty periodically glanced in her direction, watching as she efficiently worked her athletic body to its limits. She heaved and hoed with as much efficiency as one of his experienced laborers. He had to admit he was taken aback.

Smudges of dirt appeared on her flawless skin after an hour of working. She stopped to request gloves at one point, which James very willingly gave to her.

"Thanks." She genuinely smiled as she accepted them from him.

"No worries," he flirted back with his snow white smile sparkling in the sun.

Ty cleared his throat and they continued the great progress they were making.

As the morning progressed, Grace continued to banter with the guys, laughing at James' jokes, commenting on Jason's complaints, and offering her own tried and true stories to Quinn. She seemed to be accepted by all of the guys—well, almost all of the guys.

Ty, steadfast in his ways, refused to allow any sort of relationship to blossom between the two of them.

Women are bad news.

When twelve o'clock came around, everyone was thankful for the break. The site was abuzz with men getting their lunches and settling for the scheduled thirty minutes of meal time, knowing another concrete truck was on its way. Ty took another glance at Grace and saw that she sat alone by the edge of the river without food.

"You didn't bring your lunch?" he asked as he took a seat next to her on the wave break.

"Nope. It's okay. I'll eat when I get home," she smiled with her gaze facing outward toward the water.

"You can't go all day without eating," he said. Someone working as hard as she was in the heat could easily pass out.

"I'll be fine."

"Here, eat half of my sandwich. I've got enough," he handed her half of a turkey sandwich.

"Let me guess, your wife made your lunch?" Grace retorted, accepting the sandwich.

"Wife?" He half-grunted, half-laughed. "Um, no."

"You made this yourself?"

"Yeah, why? Is something wrong? Because I don't have to share."

"No! No. It's just so well put together. I mean, I know it's just a sandwich, but it looks like something you'd get at a restaurant. It looks like you cooked and carved the turkey yourself." She took several bites of the exquisite sandwich.

"Because I did."

"That's what I mean. What guy cooks his own lunch meat?"

"Me. Since I live alone, I have lots of leftovers. So I find multiple uses for them."

"I see that."

"So, what's wrong with a guy making a good meal?"

"Nothing. I'm not saying there's anything wrong. I'm just surprised. That's all."

"Well, get used to being surprised," he retorted before abandoning her at the wave break and making his way back to his truck.

He'd tried. He'd really tried. This was one woman to steer clear of.

Later that evening, Ty decided to go into town for a beer. After the day he'd had of concrete and digging, he needed something to calm down.

"Ty? What the hell are you doing here?" James yelled when

Ty walked through the aged bar door, as if his appearance was unheard of in the small, dimly lit establishment.

"Probably the same reason you're here. Work sucks and home is boring," he answered, shaking James' callused hand.

James lifted his current beer bottle to toast Ty's wisdom and chugged back a large swig before slamming the bottle pointedly back down on the bar, which got the young and clearly available bartender's attention.

Ty smiled an apology to her and hesitantly took a seat on the wooden barstool next to James.

"What can I getcha?" she cooed, her bleached hair dropping in front of her eyes.

He flashed a smile and ordered a beer. She handed it to him with a mirrored smile.

"Thanks," Ty politely replied, taking the beer from her slender hand.

"You're very welcome." She winked before turning her attention to someone else at the other end of the bar.

"Now, you've gotta get some of that," James slurred next to him.

"How much have you had to drink?"

"After today, not enough. But we're off the clock, so you can't tell me what to do."

Ty chuckled. Just as he opened his mouth to retort, a familiar brunette took the seat next to him.

"I agree with that," Grace announced, brushing her shoulder playfully against Ty.

Shit.

Ty studied her for a moment, unable to compose a reply. Her hair was casually pulled back into a ponytail, showing off more of her flawless face. She wore cut-off jean shorts and a simple white t-shirt with a Daytona Beach logo on the front. She looked hot.

Ty turned uncomfortably in his seat. "And with that, I

leave." He slapped a ten-dollar bill on the bar and stood. He couldn't handle her right now. She annoyed him, yet with her in those shorts, he wanted to take her into the back room.

"Why?" Grace challenged him.

Why, indeed?

"Look, I've had a long day. I just need a break."

"So take a break. Why do you think I'll spoil that?"

"Because I'll say something wrong and regret it in the morning," he admitted, turning on his heel and leaving the bar.

He needed space. Women were bad news.

DINNER AND A MOVIE

*S*tunned, Grace remained on the barstool next to Ty, her focus on the beer in her hands so she didn't appear affected by his sudden departure. She didn't want James to witness the breakdown of confidence she was feeling. She waited several moments, ensuring Ty was completely out the door before taking her rightful place behind the bar.

"That was just downright rude," James announced, his words somewhat slurred as he lifted his glass in salute to Grace.

She just smiled at him.

He ended his salute with a thud of the bottle on the bar. Grace grabbed a towel and wiped the counter in front of Ty's seat, removing any trace of him and collected the money he left.

She warded off any thoughts that invaded her calm, focusing on cleaning the bar.

"You going to clean that until the poly is off?" Julie asked.

"Sorry, I got lost in thought."

She collected the empty beer bottle from James.

"Want another?"

"Sure, why not? As long as I have your company."

She smiled, rolling her eyes. James was harmless and she enjoyed the casual banter they shared. It was a stark contrast from her college boyfriend, Ben. Ben was not much for small talk and didn't really take the time to converse with Grace.

Popping off the cap, Grace handed another beer to James.

"What's up with Ty? Did I do something?" she casually asked.

"Ah, he's all sorts of fucked up since Stephanie left him."

"Stephanie?"

"His ex. They were together forever. Then they weren't."

An older man and woman came into the bar and took a seat by James. Grace poured a drink for them then continued her chat with James.

"Does he know I work here?"

"I don't think so. I don't even think he figured it out tonight," James chugged down his beer. Then he added, "Why do you care anyway?"

Grace contemplated James' comment.

Why did she care? It wasn't like she owed him anything.

"I don't know. I guess I just want everyone to like me."

"Well, I like you."

Heat rushed to her cheeks and she smiled, shaking her head.

"I like you too," she answered, unsure what else to say.

Dating was new to Grace. Ben had been her first real experience with dating and he had done things much differently.

"Let's go out tonight. Can you leave early?"

His question was so spontaneous it caused Grace to fumble and almost drop a bottle.

"Go out?"

"Yeah, why not?"

She braced herself against the counter as she considered his offer. She needed to stay and make money but going out did sound like fun.

As if he sensed her trepidation, James stood, collected his wallet and deposited money onto the counter.

"Oh, come on. I'll pay," he told her, collecting his jacket from the back of the chair.

"I can't."

"Says who? It's not busy and I think your partner in crime can handle it." James pointed to Julie, who was attending to another customer on the opposite end of the bar.

Grace entertained the idea a little more as she wiped down the counter where James' beer had condensed.

"Sure, why not."

James did a little arm jerk to animate his excitement.

"I'll be outside smoking."

She briskly cleared off her side of the bar and settled tabs with the older couple before taking her leave.

"Julie, I'm going to leave early. That okay?"

Julie just smiled over her shoulder and returned to her own patrons.

Grace went to the small backroom to collect her purse and car keys, checked the bar one last time then left. James was where he promised with a half lit cigarette in his hand. The moment he spotted her he threw the cigarette down and snuffed it out with his foot then approached her.

"Where are we going?"

"Wanna come to my place? Watch a movie?" he suggested.

"How about we go *out* to a movie?"

"Or that. Drive together or separate?"

"Separate, so I can go straight home," Grace answered.

"Okay."

Grace slid behind the steering wheel of her car, taking care not to leave her phone out of reach. Not that it mattered, no one called her, but she learned to do it anyway.

The movie theater was moments from the bar and it wasn't

crowded, partly because it was Friday night and partly because there weren't any new movies out.

Grace pulled into a spot right next to James and climbed out when he opened the door for her.

"Thank you."

"You're welcome."

They entered the theater together and stood in front of the box office screen, reviewing the movie options.

"Well, the choices are horror, romance or cheesy sci-fi." Grace pointed to the wall as she categorized each movie.

"Doesn't matter to me," James said.

"Well, I'm not a fan of horror. So it's either romance or sci-fi."

"Let's go with sci-fi. We aren't ready for romance yet." His smile was goofy and awkward as he stepped to the desk and asked the young attendant for two tickets.

At least they agreed they were nowhere close to romance.

The movie didn't turn out to be so bad and it did have a romantic plot but James' humor was so appropriate it made the whole movie feel stress free and easy. James didn't pre-lecture her about inapt behaviors like Ben used to. He didn't expect her to sit a certain way or question her on how she felt about certain uncomfortable scenes. James was polite and simple, sharing his popcorn and laughing when scenes became too intimate.

It was refreshing and a nice change to the uphill battle she'd been facing since she'd graduated college.

When the movie ended, James stood and allowed Grace to lead the way out of the auditorium. He was a gentleman every step of the way, reaching around her to open doors and offering her an additional snack for the drive home.

"I'm glad I came," Grace admitted when they reached her car.

"Me too. I mean, I'm glad you came too."

"Thanks for inviting me."

"Anytime," James replied.

Grace stood there, bracing the door as a shield. Her face heated as his came closer.

This was it.

The kiss.

She felt the stubble of his beard tickle her upper lip as his lips brushed hers. It was a simple kiss, without much passion but enough to label their trip to the movies a 'date'. "Good night," he told her, stepping back to allow her to get in her car.

"Good night."

FINDING HER PLACE

Ty came in and out of vivid dreams that night as his mind sparred with Grace. In one dream, Mr. Evans carelessly fired him. In another, her expectant eyes taunted him, threatening his peace in ways he couldn't and didn't want to imagine. Why was he even thinking about her? She was just a silly girl who thought she had more authority than she actually had.

But she was the boss' daughter, after all.

Maybe making her work hard wasn't a smart move.

Shit.

Ty arrived at the site an hour early the following morning, hot coffee in his thermos and wrinkles in his Evans' Construction polo. There was no point in lying in bed if his mind wouldn't allow him to sleep.

As he wandered around the site creating a list of to-do items for the day, his mind continually roamed back to thoughts of Grace: her long, sleek legs and her bright smile. Her highlighter colored blue eyes taunted him and made his gut ache.

Stop it, Ty! He chastised himself. He couldn't be distracted, not now, not by a woman like her.

Frustrated, he grunted out loud and shook his head, trying to get the ruthless thoughts away from his mind. It had been years since a woman had gotten under Ty's skin, and he didn't like the feeling one bit.

He had drastically changed his life for the last woman he was with. He had hoped that his tireless efforts at work would prove that he had stability in his life, so if and when he was ready to get married and have children, they would have a safe and financially secure future.

Stephanie had ended their relationship, after five committed years, with a cold statement.

"Ty, I'm sorry. But I think you need to grow up and become a man."

And now, all of his hard work was being threatened again by the delicious woman who showed up unannounced with a determined drive to take over.

Did she want to take the business from him, take away everything he had worked years for?

Ty didn't want to work in the field until he retired. He aspired to move into the office and run the show from behind a clean desk. He wanted to become the boss. And Mr. Evans had made plans to ensure that Ty's aspirations would come true.

Now Grace, with her smart looks and spark of determination, was threatening to take all of that away. What was he going to prove to Stephanie then?

He needed to talk to Bill. He understood she was Bill's daughter, but he wasn't going down without a fight, damn it.

Ty sipped his hot coffee and studied the plans draped on the hood of his truck. The site was quiet. A warm breeze came off the water and ruffled the freshly planted palm trees as the moon continued to cast shadows on the ground.

"What a difference this park will make when it's complete."

Grace's vibrant voice startled him, and he almost spilled his coffee as he stepped back with a start. Then he swung around to face her.

"What the hell are you doing here this early?"

God, why did she have to look so hot? He needed to stay focused and get rid of her. But she smelled like a fresh summer flower and clean scented soap. Damn it, why was he even noticing that?

"I was about to ask you the same thing," she replied with a smile on her face. She never wavered or showed if she felt intimidated, like a guard at the Buckingham Palace.

Her hair was pulled back into a loose ponytail, and it swayed behind her as she spoke, mesmerizing Ty for a moment. Stephanie never looked so naturally beautiful, so effortless.

"I'm here to get things ready for the day," he informed her and turned his attention back to the plans.

"I thought I'd come and get a better grasp of things, so I wouldn't seem as clueless as I was yesterday," she admitted. She turned away from him, and Ty instinctively eyed her firm bottom. She wore jeans again, and they hugged all the lines of her well-etched curves.

"Look, Ty, I know you don't want me here—"

"Let's make one thing clear. Just because you're the boss' daughter doesn't mean I'm going to step down quietly," he warned her as he took another sip of his coffee.

"Who said you were stepping down?" She took a step toward him.

"Oh, come on. You said so yourself that you're here to—how'd you word it—keep the business in the family. Where does that leave me?"

"Ty, I'm not trying to take your job. The guys told me how devoted you are."

"The guys don't know shit about me."

That was true. He was a recluse, but they didn't understand

why. They speculated that he was gay or had some other problem. Besides, in the end, it was no one's business but his own.

"I can see why they don't know you," she snapped. "You're
just a tight-fisted, angry man."

Ty stopped short for a moment and collected himself. He
didn't want to spew out a list of nasty words. "And I'm leaving
it that way. Now, if you're sticking around, we might as well
make use of the time we have before the guys arrive. The
turbidity barrier broke lose. I'll need you, Quinn, and James in
the water."

Ty waited for her to complain, or at least remind him who
she was, but she didn't and Ty regretted his decision to place
her in the river the moment he saw unadulterated lust cross
James' face an hour later. James didn't hide his appraisal of
Grace's body either, and Ty almost felt embarrassed for her.

He thought placing her in the water, which most guys
would have balked at, would have scared her away. Instead, she
accepted the dirty job without qualm and jumped right into the
water to help James. Now the guy was obviously struggling to
keep his composure as they worked in the deep water that
soaked their clothes.

Hell, even Ty found it hard to focus.

Her Evans' Construction t-shirt went a deeper shade of
gray, and it clung to her body like melted chocolate to a strawberry. She moved about in the water showing no reaction to
the obvious shift in mood among the men within close prox-
imity of her.

She can't be that naive, Ty thought.

But she kept going with no hesitation or attempt to cover
herself up.

At the end of that very long day, Ty's phone rang as he was
closing the tailgate of his truck. It was Bill Evans. All of the
guys had left moments ago, and Grace was in the porta-john
changing her clothes.

"Hey, Bill, what's up?" Ty answered, surveying the site for Grace. She hadn't returned.

"Ty, I need you to come to the office tomorrow morning."

"Okay. Is everything all right?"

"Yeah, yeah. I just have a couple of things to go over with you. Grace can run the site while you're here. I've already talked to her."

Ty's heart sank. They spoke? What did they talk about? Had she complained to her father about him?

"No problem. I'll see you in the morning," Ty answered.

Shit. Shit. What was going to happen? Ty's mind went rampant with ideas. Would he get fired?

He hung up the phone and placed it back on his hip.

"Everything okay?" Grace asked from behind, catching Ty off guard again.

"Yeah. I've gotta run to the office in the morning. But you already knew that."

"Yeah, my dad told me. I'll keep things under control here." She smiled.

Did her smile seem flirty? She wouldn't be flirting if she had gotten him in trouble. Would she?

"James will be here too," Ty said, turning his back to her and heading to the cab of his truck. "Let's go. I'm ready to go home."

"Then go. I'll finish up here," she said and walked away from his truck.

"I can't. I have to lock the gate after you," he said from his driver's seat. His power intact.

"Oh, right. Give me the keys anyway. I need them so I can get in tomorrow morning," she called after him and returned to the cab of his truck at a brisk run.

Oh God. Don't run. Please don't run. Too many bad thoughts.

"James has a set. He can open it in the morning."

Grace smiled, accepted defeat with dignity and walked back

to her car. She provided him with one last mocking smile before closing her door.

They didn't exchange words as Ty locked the gate and left; each of them driving in a different direction.

FRIENDLY CHAT

*L*ater that night James came to the bar, his mood somewhat down.

"What's up?" Grace placed a beer in front of him without request.

"Nothing. Just tired. Today wiped me out."

"Yeah, me too."

James took a long chug of his beer and hunched over the bar. He wasn't much for conversation so Grace turned her attention to other patrons she was serving.

"Another?" she asked an older woman who was apparently waiting for a date that hadn't arrived.

"Yeah." The woman responded, defeat in her tone.

"How late is he?" Grace asked.

"An hour."

"This one's on me then."

Grace poured the woman another rum and coke then returned her attention to James.

"Sore?"

"Hell yeah. You?"

"Yeah. I don't have to close tonight, so I'm going to soak in a hot bath when I get home."

"Sounds like a plan. Wanna come over to my place instead? I've got a hot tub."

Of course, he would. What bachelor wouldn't?

Grace paused her cleaning ritual.

"Nothing sexual. I promise. Just two friends hanging out," he clarified.

Well, if he put it that way.

"Sure, why not. It's not like I have something better to do."

Grace closed out her tab, cleaned the bar and said her good-byes to Julie before following James out the door for the second night in a row.

After getting an address from James and collecting her bathing suit, she followed the map on her phone down the various roads to an older, yet well maintained, neighborhood and pulled into a driveway of a simple modest house with low maintenance landscaping and neutral paint colors.

Grace never actually stepped foot into the house that night. The Jacuzzi was behind the detached two-car garage on an elevated deck and the bathroom was in the back of the garage so there was no need to go into the house at all.

The deck itself was newly constructed, with Tiki torches and a Tiki themed bar off to the right. Grace could tell James was an entertainer from the first day they met and seeing his backyard cemented that impression.

"Wanna beer?"

"No thanks. I'm not much of a beer drinker."

"Oh. Okay. How about wine? I've got a bottle in the house somewhere."

"No thanks. You can get a beer for yourself though."

James departed with zest, either sprinting to return as quickly as he could or because he really wanted a beer.

Ben never drank. He used to say, "Drinking clouds your senses and I want to be of sound mind with everything I do with you." At first, Grace thought it was romantic, the amount of attention he placed on her, but then it weighed on her, controlling her and making her uncomfortably conscious of everything she did.

James returned beer in hand, and jumped into the hot tub next to her, the water moving in waves across the surface.

"Ah, that's nice."

"I agree." Grace giggled as the water sloshed around them.

"I wish Ty agreed to come over."

"You asked Ty to come."

"Yeah, why not? He usually comes over."

"And what did he say?"

"He's been in a pissy mood. I asked and he just shook his head and made some lame excuse about work to do at home."

"Do you think it's because of me?"

"You? No. He just needs to get laid."

Grace laughed, the sound bouncing around the backyard and back to her ears.

"Well, I can't very well help with that."

"No, you can't. Speaking of relationships…" James paused, "Do you have a boyfriend?"

The question came from so far left field it took Grace a moment to re-center herself.

Why was he asking that now? Hadn't their kiss last night answered that question?

"Me? No, I don't. Actually, I broke up with my last boyfriend over a year ago."

"Oh, what happened?"

"It's a long story. Let's just say he hurt me and I needed to move on."

"Fair enough."

"What about you?" Grace asked.

"Me? I'm single but not really looking. Just having fun." He draped his arms around the seats beside him.

"Well, at least you know where you stand."

"Yeah. Oh, by the way, this is way off topic, but I am planning a Halloween party and you really need to come. We have a blast every year. It'll be the shit, with music and drinks and I even have a costume contest."

"Sounds like fun."

"It is. It'll be epic. You've gotta come."

"Sure," Grace agreed.

They continued to talk well into the night about various topics that really didn't have value or merit. Grace enjoyed the light conversation and easy candor that she was developing with James. He was such a contrast to Ben.

When the clock struck midnight, Grace announced she needed to go.

James walked her to her car, opening the door so Grace could get in. She turned to face him again, expecting another pleasant kiss. James must have been in harmony because he positioned himself so they could enjoy another. His beard tickled her upper lip again, a feeling she knew would remain on her lips for some time after the kiss ended. James was polite and ended the kiss at the appropriate time.

"Thanks for coming." James placed his hands on her hips.

"Thanks for having me." She smiled.

"Drive safe." He put his hand on the door so she could climb inside.

"I will." She started the car and put on her seatbelt.

"See you in the morning." He waved goodbye as she pulled away.

He waved as she backed out of his driveway.

James was proving to become a positive addition to her shitty life. It was about time.

MEETING WITH DAD

*T*y wore his best clothes and spent extra time shaving the next morning. He needed Mr. Evans to know he was serious. He didn't want to lose his job to a woman, let alone lose the company. He'd worked too hard for that.

Smelling crisp and clean in his neatly ironed shirt, he arrived at the office at least ten minutes earlier than everyone else. Ty prided himself for always being ahead of schedule. He carried his hot coffee, an essential part of his mornings, into the very still office.

"Bill?" Ty called out when he stepped through the door.

"Yeah?" His boss called from the back office, his strong voice carrying through the building like a drum.

"I'm here. Where do you want me?"

"Come back here!"

Ty swallowed a large mouthful of air and walked briskly to Bill's office, careful to not slosh his coffee from the little hole in the lid. The light was on, and Bill was sitting at his desk, squinting at the computer screen.

Bill was an older man whose life in construction clearly

showed in his gray hair and well worked hands. He wasn't one to run the business solely behind his desk. He still picked up a tool every so often and swung a hammer to ensure his employees knew he was serious.

"I hate these damn things," Bill said. An old-fashioned business owner, Bill resisted technology. He would moan and groan about email and having to type proposals in a computer program too complex for anyone to fully understand.

"What do you need help with?" Ty offered.

"It's this damn file. I pressed Save, and now I can't find it." Bill squinted a little deeper. His large fingers scrolled frantically on the mouse wheel.

"Try recent files," Ty suggested as he leaned over the desk to look at the screen.

Bill clicked a couple of times.

"Aha! There it is!" Bill's face lit up. "These damn new computers. Just when I get the old ones figured out, they go and change them on me."

Ty smiled. "I bet Karen can give you a tutorial." He laughed as he took a seat in one of the plush chairs in front of Bill's desk.

"She has, several times. But this damn thing is so confusing." Bill motioned to the very new and obviously expensive computer. "Anyway, that's not why I wanted you to come here." Bill leaned back in his chair. "I wanted to talk about Grace."

"What about Grace?"

Bill let out a sigh and rolled his eyes. "That little girl of mine is determined to run this business." He paused, and Ty waited. "She's so damn independent."

"Well, that's how you raised her. That's something you should be proud of."

Bill looked up at Ty and shook his head. "When you have kids, you'll understand what I'm about to say." Bill sat up in the chair and placed his elbows on the desk. "Grace is a pain in my ass."

Ty laughed loudly in relief.

"It's true," Bill said. "If you tell her to walk straight, she will purposely walk in circles to prove that both are ways to get from A to B."

"Yeah, I could see that." Ty thought of her attempt to hide behind a tree to change her clothes.

"I bet you could. What was she wearing when she arrived at the site on Monday?"

"Um." Ty fumbled for the right words.

"It's all right. I'm not going to fire you because you looked at my daughter. Was she wearing a dress? Heels?"

"Well, shorts. Yeah, heels."

"I knew it. I told her not to dress up. She argued with me that she needed to present herself in a professional manner so the guys would take her seriously." Bill put air quotes around 'professional'.

"Well, they definitely," Ty gulped and searched for the right words without offending, "made an impression."

"I bet they ogled her. I'm not stupid. My daughter is a good-looking woman. But she doesn't belong in construction. I don't want her in construction."

"In her defense, she did have jeans and boots in her car."

"That damn girl. See what I mean?" Bill threw his arms up.

"Yeah. I know exactly what you mean." He laughed nervously.

"Don't worry. You're getting this company. I love my daughter, and that's why I don't want her stepping into my role. She'll run herself into the ground. Construction is a man's world. I want her to be happy. But we've gotta get Grace to give up her dream." Bill leaned back into his seat again.

"We?"

"The sooner she realizes that she can't run this company, the sooner I can retire and live out my final days in peace. I want you to sit in this chair, not her. You can run this company. You've got it in you. I want you to make her work, make her uncomfortable, make her want to change her mind and follow a different career path."

"I don't know." He couldn't help thinking Grace did have a right to choose what she wanted, after all, even if it meant he would have to step down.

"Look, just make her work. Trust me. I know my daughter. She'll give up in a couple of weeks."

Ty ARRIVED at the job site shortly after his meeting with Mr. Evans and immediately sought out Grace. He found her with some of the guys, but none of them was working. She was laughing at something one of the laborers had said.

"Oh, good morning, Ty. How'd your meeting go?" she politely asked and stood up to approach him with her bouncy hair pulled back again in a ponytail.

Wouldn't you like to know?

"Good. It went much better than I expected," he said. Then he turned his attention to the workers. "Let's get this thing on the road. No time to sit." He continued to bark orders until all of the men were occupied with tasks.

Grace stood purposely by his side without saying a word as she studied his leadership. When work was finally in full swing, Ty turned to her.

"I thought the men would be working when I arrived," he said, actively working to keep his eyes focused on the site. He hoped it would portray his disappointment.

She shifted her weight from one hip to the other, her body

going rigid and her eyes shining annoyed anger. She didn't speak at first, just defiantly placed her hands on her hips and glared at him.

"I didn't know what the game plan was."

"A good superintendent would have taken action to figure it out, to ensure progress on a job site is not hindered."

"You're right. But communication is another trait of a good superintendent." She grabbed a shovel that leaned against the job trailer and walked back toward some of the laborers.

What the hell is that supposed to mean?

To Ty's amazement, she got right to work, digging a trench alongside his laborers.

That damn woman.

Ty rolled his eyes and turned his attention to the electrician, who, in turn, diverted his mind from her for the next several hours.

Periodically, Ty caught himself looking in her direction and studying her as her molded muscles flexed and released with each thrust she put into the shovel. Single strands of hair started to wiggle their way out of her neat ponytail, and as the minutes turned into hours, her face flushed with exhaustion.

She never once stopped or complained. Some of the men working around her stopped to smoke cigarettes and eye her as well. She kept working. Her body swayed with the swings of the shovel. Her Evans' Construction t-shirt had become damp with perspiration.

"Let's break for lunch!" Ty called across the property when the clock struck noon. Shovels hit the ground almost immediately.

As much as Ty didn't want to admit it, he promptly looked for her small figure. He had worked her hard that day and felt a little pang of guilt over it.

He wanted her gone in more ways than he could express,

but at the same time, there was a small part of him that liked having her around—a really, really small part.

She had grabbed her bright pink lunch box and made her way to the river's shoreline.

"How are you doing?" he asked, approaching her with his own lunch box.

She turned to face him, smiling to be polite, but clearly exhausted.

"Great. It's a good workout," she told him. She took a bite of her turkey sandwich.

Bullshit.

"Are you really—" His fingers made air quotes. "Great?"

"Yup." She took another bite and kept her focus on the water.

"Look, about this morning—"

"There's nothing to say. You're the man in charge. I get it. I'm stepping on your toes. And my father basically told you to get rid of me. I'm not stupid," she told him as she finished her sandwich.

"Grace, you've just got to understand, this is my job at stake too."

"How is your job at stake? My dad has told me for years that you're the best. I know he's giving the company to you." She stood to walk away.

"Exactly. And you made it clear that you want to take it."

"Of course, I do. And I have every right to want to," Grace explained.

"You're right. But he doesn't want you to have it."

"I know that. And that's why I'm here busting my ass to prove to him that I won't fail."

"I've busted my ass for ten years," Ty said.

"Good for you. And I intend to keep you because of your loyalty."

"I don't want to be a loyal employee. I want to be the boss."

"Well, so do I. And I deserve a chance since I'm his daughter," Grace said.

"Yup, I guess the spoiled get what they want while the rest of us get screwed."

Ty regretted the line the moment it stung past his lips. He had gone too far, and he knew it.

"Is that what you think of me? That I'm just some spoiled brat that gets anything I want?" Grace asked.

"I do. And you're mad that Daddy won't let you have this too," Ty threw out.

She froze, her reaction unreadable. An audience was gathering now.

"You have no clue what my life is like," she spat angrily.

Before he could respond, she turned on her heel and stomped her tiny feet back to her car. She got in, starting it effortlessly and peeled out onto the road carelessly into oncoming traffic.

Ty looked around at his men as they stared back with their jaws dropped.

"What?" Ty shouted. "Get back to work; there's nothing to see here!" He threw his hands up in the air as they all scurried back to work.

James lingered as Ty paced nervously like a caged lion.

"I fucked up, didn't I?" Ty asked him with a shake of his head.

"Yup. You really have no clue."

"What's that supposed to mean?"

"Ty, she's living in a motel," James said.

"What?"

"She's living in a motel on Ridgewood Avenue. She's working nights at the Bar to make money."

"What? Why?"

"You really have no clue." James shook his head and walked away.

Ty stood there for a minute and chewed on that. How had James known this, and why hadn't he?

She was living at a motel, and a really crappy one at that. Her father hadn't said anything about that. Wasn't he aware of her situation? And why the hell hadn't someone told him that sooner?

APOLOGY

*G*race reached the light at the intersection with white knuckles on the steering wheel. She was afraid if she let go she'd break the window beside her.

"Agh!" she screamed out, hoping the release would make her feel better.

The light turned green, and she stomped her foot on the pedal which launched the car into the intersection. The man next to her sped up to pass her, and she stomped on the gas to blow past him.

"Stupid men."

She arrived at her father's office in the shortest amount of time ever. She slammed the car door, strode up to the office, and thrust open the storefront door.

Karen greeted her with a smile. "Good afternoon, Grace."

"Good afternoon, Karen. Is my father here?"

"He is, but he's on the phone."

"No problem. I'll have a seat in front of him. Thanks." She briskly walked back to his office.

Her father was leaning back in his chair, pinching the bridge of his nose as he talked on the phone.

"Jerry, all I need from you is a set of plans," he was saying when she threw her body into the chair in front of his desk.

He didn't react to her sudden appearance, not even cracking a smile. "Look, someone just arrived for my next appointment. We'll have to discuss this another time," he said, then listened for a minute. "That's fine. Just get them done. Okay? Bye." He hung up, then paused briefly.

"Look, I already know what happened," he said.

"Do you now? And who told you?"

"Ty."

"Ty? Really. And what did Ty have to say?" She crossed her arms over her chest and leaned forward.

"He told me that he said a couple of choice things that were offensive and he would like to apologize for them." He crossed his fingers over each other.

"Apologize!" She let out a laugh.

"Yes, apologize."

"I think it's too late for that."

"Grace," he paused again. "This is exactly why I've told you that you don't belong in construction."

"Now you sound like Ty!"

"We both know you tend to use bad judgment. This is one of those times. You can't be out there swinging a hammer with the guys. You could hurt yourself."

"Seriously, Dad? My judgment?"

He rolled his eyes and lounged back into his thick leather chair.

"I'm not having this discussion with you again. Remember, Ben?"

"Oh, here we go again. Do you honestly think I haven't forgotten? You won't let me. But it's been a year and I've done more than my share to prove that I learned from my mistakes."

"Have you?"

"Yeah. I have. So for once in your life, trust me. Let me show you that I can do this."

"Grace. I'll trust you when you're home picking a career more suited for a woman."

"And that's exactly why I refuse to come home. It's not the nineteenth century. Women can do anything men can do. So get off that."

"Grace. Please. I don't have time for this."

Grace couldn't think of a clever response, so settled with, "You know what; I'll prove both you and Ty wrong if it's the last thing you see me do!"

"Grace, stop!"

"No. I'm not going to stop. It's not costing you a dime for me to be there, so I'll keep going until both of you realize that a woman can do a man's job." She stood, jamming her dirtied pointer finger onto his desk.

"Grace. Please."

"No, Dad. I have a job. Right here in your company. And I'll be damned if he gets it."

With that she turned on her heel and left.

PROPOSAL

$\mathcal{J}$y pulled his pickup truck into a parking spot outside the bar after the day exhausted his emotions and tested every bit of patience he had left. The moon was high and the air was a warm blanket. He checked his reflection in the rearview mirror, let out a painful breath, and climbed down. The neon lights buzzed above his head as he opened the front door for a woman approaching to leave. He stepped to the side, held the door open, and waited until she cleared the doorway.

"Thank you," she smiled as she sidestepped through.

"You're welcome."

He found an open stool at the bar and slid in unnoticed.

He looked around the room, hoping to see the familiar brunette head he was searching for. He felt a little pang of disappointment when she wasn't immediately spotted. The usual bleach-blonde bartender approached him.

"What can I get for ya?" she asked, smacking her gum between her lips. She bent down, elbows on the bar to expose the tops of her round breasts.

"Is Grace working tonight?" he politely asked as he looked down at the bartender.

"Yeah. I think she's outside. I can getcha what you need. We share tips." She pursed her lips, pushed her elbows closer together on the bar, and forced her breasts forward.

"No thanks. I just need to talk to Grace."

She straightened herself from the bar and gave him a once over before turning away. Ty sat for a few minutes, waiting for her to return. He turned his attention to the football game on the television above the bar.

She returned alone.

"I don't know whatcha did, but she doesn't want to talk to you," she announced with a smile.

"Oh, come on," he huffed out. "Can I go out back to see her?"

"Whoa, buddy. She doesn't want to talk to you, so the answer's no." She reached out and placed her hand, with fake, bright green fingernails, on his chest to stop him from moving any further.

"Fine. Please tell her I said I'm sorry." He sighed and turned to leave.

"Whatcha do anyways? She won't tell me."

"I said some mean things."

"That's it? And she's going to let a hunk like you walk out the door because you said some mean things? What's wrong with that girl?"

"They were pretty nasty words."

"I'll talk to her," she told him, holding up an excessively long fingernail.

Ty turned back to the bar and reclaimed his seat. Maybe she could help his cause. After a few moments Grace appeared from the back door.

Thank you, bartender.

She had changed into skimpy jean shorts that showcased her beautiful legs. Ty suddenly felt a pang of possession and the need to cover her up so other guys in the bar wouldn't notice her. Her slightly tanned legs were shaven smooth, and the logo t-shirt she wore was tight across her well-endowed chest and tied in a knot at the base of her back.

"Look, Ty," she said with a hand propped on her hip. "I'm working right now and don't have time to reminisce about our little encounter earlier today."

For some odd reason it felt as if Ty held a magnifying glass in his hands, and he was noticing all the small things about her he hadn't noticed before.

Her brown hair was cut so that the ends wisped into fine curls as it hung freely down her back. Her cheeks held a light stain, and her teeth were as white as crisp, clean snow.

"I screwed up. When do you get off? I'd really like to talk about this," he asked her with a deep pleading in his eyes.

"When do I get off?" Her fine eyebrows creased in question and small pleats developed around her petite nose.

"Yeah, when does your shift end?"

"Does it matter? I don't want to talk to you." Her hand landed awkwardly back on her hip.

"Hey," Ty summoned the bartender over to them. "What time does her shift end?"

She looked at Grace then answered, "Two a.m." She smiled at Grace before retreating to her drunken patrons at the bar.

"Then I'll be back at two."

She just shook her head, turned, and walked away.

Ty pulled his truck next to Grace's car at the back of the bar promptly at two a.m..

Just as he turned the key, the back door opened, and out walked Grace.

She was smiling at something her fellow bartender was telling her, and her whole face lit up with unadulterated joy. This was something Ty hadn't witnessed as of yet. For the short moment she enjoyed her laugh, Grace looked beautiful. Pure. She released the knot at her waist and the t-shirt unfolded around her hips, covering the small ring he'd seen in her belly button earlier.

Her smile faded when she noticed him. Ty got out of his truck and walked toward her.

"Ty, seriously?"

The wrinkles at the bottom of her shirt caught his attention. Not because they were messy but because the length of the t-shirt hid the hem of her shorts and it appeared like she was only wearing the shirt. That simple observation triggered another side of Ty's mind, a side he really didn't want activated right now.

He felt a tinge of disappointment that her anger hadn't disappeared.

"I feel awful for what I said, and would really like the chance to make it up to you," he answered as he opened her car door for her.

She flung her purse into the passenger seat and stepped behind the door.

"There's no need to talk. You apologized before. Just go home."

"No. Not until we talk. I screwed up. I've gotta make this right," he continued, while holding the door open. He stood to the side, allowing her room to climb in but didn't make an effort to close the door.

"Grace?" a man's voice from the back of the building called out.

"I'm fine, Joe!" she called back.

Ty kept his attention on Grace and kept the door open so they could continue to talk.

"I'm sorry for being an ass."

"It's fine, Ty. I get it. You can go home now. My dad won't fire you."

"I'm not worried about your father."

"Ty, seriously. I'm tired. I just want to go home."

Then something in Ty clicked and a light filled cloud of realization showered over him.

"Why are you working two jobs?"

"Why? Because my dad doesn't think I can run his business. Apparently, that spot has been reserved for you." She placed her delicate fingers on the steering wheel, her eyes trained on them.

"Your dad won't support you if you continue to stay in construction?"

"Who says I need his support? I'm doing just fine on my own." She flashed a glance at him and then returned her attention to her hands.

"Why don't you come back to my place, and we'll talk?" he blurted out, the words sounding more desperate than he intended.

He really didn't want Joe, or the other bartender, or anyone else for that matter involved in their conversation anymore. As he stood there, the streetlight over Grace's car casting a halo of light, illuminating her face, Ty thought about Stephanie. Thought about how ruthless she was at the end of their relationship by telling him he was unstable, worthless, and had no potential.

"Whatcha going to do the rest of your life? Be a laborer, doing grunt work every day? How will that support us if we have children?" she'd challenged him one night.

Now, years later, he'd made someone else feel as low as Stephanie had made him feel that night. He had to repent. He had to take it back. He was a better man than that.

"I can't. I've got a long day tomorrow." She brushed him off and tried to close the door. Her arm barely touching his sent a wave of awareness down his entire arm.

"Please. I know what you're going through."

"Do you? Do you have any clue what it's like to have everyone around you tell you that you'll fail and that you don't belong?"

"Yes, I do. I proposed to a girl, and the same night she left me she said it was because I was a failure."

RUNNING ON E

$\mathcal{G}$race was startled for a moment, grasping the reality of his confession. She honestly didn't see that coming. Ty didn't strike her as the kind of guy who would be left at the altar.

"I'm sorry." She released the door so he could continue to hold it and talk to her.

"Don't be. What's happened, happened. I can't change it." He straightened his posture.

"How can you be so positive?" She placed both of her hands on the steering wheel and turned to him.

"Positive? I wouldn't call it positive. I can't change it so why dwell on it?" He sounded so insightful, it impressed her.

"I wish I could sound that positive." She turned to look out the windshield.

"You can. You've just got to decide what is right for you and do it." He stepped inside the door opening and leaned down over the door sill.

"I'm trying to but everyone keeps getting in my way." She leveled with him.

"I know, and I'm sorry for that. I know how it feels. Will

you please come back to my place so we can talk? I'm not the guy you think I am. I'd really like the chance to make up for what I said."

Talk? Is that what he really wanted?

She recognized the controlling nature in Ty the day they met. In the short time they'd worked together she saw it over and over again. In a lot of ways, he was like Ben. Ben would gain control of any situation then spin it into a sexual lesson. Could she trust Ty not to do the same?

"Just talk?"

"Yeah. Just talk."

"Fine. But I need to stop and get gas. I'm practically on empty."

"That's fine. I'll follow you to the station then you can follow me home."

Ty returned to his truck then followed her to the gas station. She didn't plan on him hovering over her at the pump. She wished he had stayed in his car so she wouldn't be embarrassed as she tried each of her cards to determine which one had enough money to get gas with.

She begged her first credit card to accept the transaction. If she had five dollars available on the card it would allow her to go over.

But, as fate would have it, the screen glared declined.

Shamefully, she returned to her purse to dig out her debit card. She knew she had somewhere around seven dollars in her account.

She swiped the card and thankfully grabbed the pump when it wasn't declined.

Ty watched her with his body casually leaning against her car. He didn't say a word and Grace cringed at the thoughts she assumed were going through his mind.

"I get paid tomorrow." She fumbled with the pump as she watched the number approach the seven dollar mark. After tapping it a few times to round up the number, she returned the nozzle to its base.

"Is that enough to fill your tank?"

"No."

"Are you really that low on funds?"

She didn't want to answer, too embarrassed.

"Here. I've got this." He swiped his card and returned the nozzle to her tank.

"Seriously, you don't have to do that." She crossed her arms over her chest.

"I know, but I want to. It's the least I can do." He pressed the button and started to pump the gas.

"Now you're making me feel bad." She looked down at her feet and scuffed at the ground.

"Why?"

"Because it's not your responsibility to fill my tank." She let out a sigh.

"I never said it was." He pumped the handle a couple of times.

She took in a deep breath.

"Well, thank you. I'll pay you back tomorrow." She stepped to the side so he could return the handle to its base.

"Don't worry about it." He pressed a couple of buttons on the screen and then stepped away.

"I will. I don't like to be in anyone's pocket."

"Who said you were in my pocket?"

He replaced the nozzle when the tank was full.

"I do. I don't want a man to think he has to take care of me." She started to climb back into her car.

"Trust me. I know you're self-sufficient. Just say thank you and get back in your car." There was Ben again.

"Thanks, but next time, mind your own business." With that she closed her car door.

GROUND RULES

$\mathcal{T}$y didn't mean to get so personal but he couldn't ask her to drive all the way out to his house on seven dollars' worth of gas, which was clearly all she had.

He felt relieved when she followed him.

He'd checked his rear-view mirror as they left the gas station to make sure she was behind him. At two in the morning, there weren't many cars on the road, so it was easy for her to follow, yet Ty glanced in his rear-view mirror several times to ensure her headlights remained in view. The weak, raw side of him feared she would change her mind and turn off onto some side road before he could gather what had happened.

Why did he care so much all of the sudden?

He turned off the main boulevard and continued to his home on the rural side of town. Street lights were no longer lining the road and creating halos of light for them to pass under so Ty turned on his high beams to broaden his range of view. They passed fields and farm houses that were dark as people slept in their beds.

Ten minutes later, he signaled left to turn onto his dusty

dirt driveway leading to his ten acres. He hoped she'd like his modest house.

Why do you care if she likes your house? He asked himself as his truck crawled over the rocks that popped under the weight of his truck. A cloud of dust splayed behind him, clouding her car. He pulled into his usual spot alongside the front porch and climbed out as she pulled in behind him.

"Jeez, I was beginning to wonder if you were bringing me back here to kill me," she announced as she climbed out of her car and wrapped her arms around her scantily dressed body as the cool night air embraced her bare skin.

"Nope, this is where I live. And, as you see, it's always a lot cooler out here. Come on, let's go inside," he told her and reached out to offer his arm for warmth.

Arms crossed over her chest, she hesitantly looked around and politely rejected his arm.

Ty retracted it and led the way up the recently renovated front porch.

"Do you live alone?" she asked as she stepped into the warm house with her arms still crossed over her chest.

"Yeah."

"Isn't it lonely out here?" she asked. Her curious eyes studied his house from her vantage point just inside the door like she had a test on it tomorrow.

Ty honed in on the mask of chill-bumps covering her flawless skin.

"Here, let me get you a jacket." He left her at the door as he went to his bedroom for a jacket. Like a teenage boy bringing a girl home to a vacant house he rushed, frantically scouring his closet for something worthy enough to be worn.

Jesus. Collect yourself.

"Here you go." He returned with a large red and black flannel jacket he'd worn the day before, which he'd smelled before bringing it to her to make sure it didn't reek.

She smiled and eagerly wrapped it around her small frame. The jacket practically swallowed her. A childish smile crept on his lips.

"Thank you." She smiled, stepping further into the room.

"You're welcome. You want some coffee?" he asked rushing toward his newly renovated kitchen to busy himself before he did or said something inappropriate.

"Um, yeah. I'm usually in bed by now. Coffee might help keep me up." She stepped into the French-country kitchen, eying the curved exhaust hood and impeccable workmanship of the custom cabinetry.

"This kitchen is beautiful," she told him as she smoothed her hand along the cold granite surface of the countertop.

"Thanks. I just finished it." He pulled out two red coffee mugs from the dark maple cabinets, turning to find her closer to him.

"Did you do it all by yourself?"

"Yeah."

"It's beautiful." She studied the small details only someone in construction would notice, like how the molding wasn't purchased but hand carved and strategically placed to add to the elegance of each cabinet.

He watched her for a moment as she touched different elements of his workmanship. His oversized flannel jacket was longer than her shorts, so he could pretend it was the only thing she was wearing. Her toned legs stretched below it, drawing his attention as she walked slowly around the kitchen.

Ty courted the idea of waking up in the morning with Grace standing in his kitchen with the sun's radiance coming through the window as she wore only that jacket.

"Okay, you've shown off your house. Let's get to the point. What revelation did you want to share with me?" She placed her hand on her hip again, which forced all of her weight to one side.

Oh no! What the hell just happened?

Why did he ask her to come here again? Did she not realize what her legs were doing to him?

"Ahem!" She cleared her throat.

Oh yeah, for being a jerk today.

"Look, I'm really sorry for what I said earlier," he forced out of his mouth.

"It's fine. You didn't have to drag me all the way out to your house to say that. You're out of the dog house now," she responded, her voice lazy and unaffected. She propped her hand on her hip, as if she was expectant of more.

"No, I want you to understand that I get it. I understand why you're mad," Ty explained.

"You understand why I'm mad? Really? Because I don't think you do."

She took the mug of coffee he offered and leaned on the high counter.

"I don't want you to think that I'm sexist."

"But you are sexist, and so is my father." She took a sip of coffee, pausing as the hot liquid slipped past her tongue and down her throat.

"But I'm not sexist. It's just that—"

"I get it, Ty. I came along and threatened your job. I get it. And if I were a man, my father probably would have given the company to me. But because I'm a woman, he's refusing to give me a chance."

"You could have all the skill in the world. Women just don't belong in construction. The construction industry is full of, well, horny men. Horny men who would eat you alive if given the opportunity."

She took a step back, offense plastered to her face.

"Ty, do you want to fuck me?"

She had never spoken with such vulgarity before, so Ty took a step away. "What?"

"Do you want to fuck me?" Grace asked again.

He paused. What was he supposed to say?

"You don't have to answer, I'm not stupid. I know how the male mind works."

"I'm not like that."

"Good. Because I'm not going to have sex with you, ever."

"I never said I wanted to."

And what did she mean by 'ever'? Like never ever?

"Oh, you don't have to say anything. I can tell by how you act," Grace said.

"What? No!" Ty argued.

She straightened up, causing the jacket to gape open.

"Ty, let's get a couple of things straight. One, I'm not here to be eye candy for you or any of the guys. Two, I'm not backing down from what I want. And three, it's my right to run my father's business. So, you better get used to me, as your boss." She looked down at his crotch. "Not your next fuck."

NEIGHBORS

*G*race swallowed hard, then stripped herself of his jacket and walked out the front door. The cool air outside didn't affect her as it had before. This time, she moved with one purpose, to leave his house as fast as possible.

Men!

She didn't buckle her seatbelt before she threw the transmission in drive. The stone pebbles threw themselves against the side of her car as she departed down the dirt driveway and back out onto a more familiar country road.

She knew her hasty departure left a cloud of dust and she hoped Ty saw it as she knew he inevitably raced out onto the porch to get her.

She couldn't believe she had spoken to him the way she had. *Not your next fuck.*

It was classic. She had never spoken to anyone that way. And the most surprising thing was; it felt amazing. She had been liberated. After a six-year relationship with a man who treated her like a submissive, both in the bedroom and out, it was liberating to throw power back at someone else.

Now she understood why Ben was so intent on being in charge. Grace always thought he was in charge because he was more experienced than she. It was only natural that someone with more experience would lead the way. Except now she understood the thrill he got from having power over her.

Ben controlled everything she did, from scheduling her classes to what he expected in the bedroom. Grace had openly accepted his version of a relationship, naive and curious at the same time. It was a relief not to have to worry about anything, Ben was always in control.

Grace turned down the main road back to her motel, eager to get there and shower. She needed to clean off the layer of filth her words had exposed her to. The whole encounter had her amped up and fighting feelings she hadn't felt in a long time. Feelings that didn't belong with Ty. Boy, she really needed to settle herself so she could go to sleep.

Then she remembered her date out with the girls tomorrow.

Shit.

Grace had been back in town several weeks when her old high school girlfriends found out and planned a day out to make up for missed time. Grace had almost forgotten that day was tomorrow.

She really needed to sleep in. She could call them when she woke up and apologize.

Nah. She needed this. She needed time away from the guys and all of the drama it brought. She just wanted to have light-hearted fun out with the girls, giggling about stupid things and gossiping about their latest flings.

She pulled into the dimly lit parking lot of her motel and secured a spot closest to her room. She hated being there, hating having to live in a motel to prove herself to her father.

She knew she made mistakes. She knew she had to learn

from them, but why did she have to stoop so low to make that impression? It sucked.

The light outside her door was flickering as she placed the key in her door. She knew it was a matter of time before it went out altogether and she'd have to call the sleazy maintenance guy to come down and fix it.

Her room had its familiar musky smell and Grace reached into her purse to dig out the plug-in refills she purchased earlier that day. She may be poor, but she wouldn't suffer the stale smell of her room.

As she bent down to place the clean linen refill in the plug-in, there was a knock on her door.

Who could that be at three a.m.?

Grace grabbed for her purse, digging for her mace and approached the door, her arm stretched out in front with her thumb on the trigger.

"Who is it?"

"Your neighbor. You dropped something on your way in."

"Oh? Just leave it by the door. I'll grab it later. Thanks."

She wasn't stupid. She'd been on her own and anyone knocking at her door at three a.m. was not someone to open the door for.

"Okay. It's a key with a silver surfboard on the ring. I'll hide it behind the chair."

Shit. Her key to the bar.

It could wait until the morning.

"Thanks," she called through the door.

"You're welcome."

Just when she tried to prove how responsible she was…

Damn it.

Then she reconsidered leaving it outside. She waited about ten minutes for her neighbor to return to his room and snuck outside to retrieve it.

SEEING RED

*S*aturday morning proved to be difficult for Ty. After Grace abruptly left his house, he spent another long night staring at the ceiling, unable to relax and stop the endless thoughts spooling in his mind. He didn't get women. He hadn't asked for Grace's attention. He didn't even hit on her. She was the one who showed up at his job site.

So why was he the bad guy?

Maybe because he couldn't stop lusting after her?

Even as he struggled to get back to sleep, Ty couldn't erase the sight of her in his flannel, her sun caressed legs peaking from beneath it.

Defeated, he eventually dragged himself out of bed and haphazardly pulled on a pair of American flag shorts and a white t-shirt.

James had called moments earlier and reminded Ty about their 'date with the water'. James never missed an opportunity to be out on Ty's 18' fishing boat, suggesting they use it practically every weekend.

"Long night?" James asked when Ty answered the phone hungover from his sleepless night.

"I'll tell you when we get on the road."

Ty then brushed his teeth, groomed his hair and dismissed his five o'clock shadow before James arrived at the door. Thankfully, James offered a cup of hot coffee from Dunkin Donuts.

Ty graciously accepted it and headed outside to hook up the boat to his truck. The task was harder than usual as he slowly awoke.

"Dude? What are you doing? You're acting like you've never done this before," James commented after Ty had to back up and pull forward for the fourth time to align the hitch to the trailer.

"I'm sorry. This coffee just hasn't kicked in yet." He threw the truck into drive one more time, then reverse.

"I think you need more than coffee." James told him as he backed the truck up again.

"Dude, you have no idea." Ty successfully hitched the truck to the boat trailer and climbed back in.

"So, you going to tell me what happened?" James asked as Ty pulled out of his driveway.

"I honestly have no clue." Ty drove down the road, taking another sip of his coffee.

"Well, start with what happened." James suggested.

"I went to the bar to apologize to Grace." He stopped at a red light.

"You did?" James sounded surprised.

"Yeah, I felt bad. You were right. I judged her too soon." He drove on as the light turned green.

"And what'd she say?" James was a little more attentive now.

"She brushed me off at first. Then I got her to come back to my place." James froze in his seat, almost as if he was angry.

"What'd I say?" James didn't speak.

"Dude. What's up?" Ty tried again, lightly punching James in the arm.

"It's nothing. I just didn't realize she was unavailable." He kept his eyes fixed on the windshield.

"What the hell does that mean?" Ty asked, furrowing his eyebrows.

"Nothing, just tell me what happened." James brushed it off and continued as if the moment hadn't even happened.

"She accused me of trying to sleep with her then left."

"Did you? Try to sleep with her?" James asked, the question somewhat offensive to Ty.

"No."

"Good," James said.

"You're acting weird. What's going on?" Ty tried to focus on the road and James at the same time.

"Nothing," James replied.

The conversation ended just as they arrived at the boat launch. Ty didn't give James' reaction much more thought. Instead, he focused on the perfect weather, the warm air and the ice-cold beer that was waiting for him in the cooler.

A HALF-HOUR later he stood in front of the captain's chair: shamelessly shirtless, driving down the wide river, ready to drink the day away. His black sunglasses shielded his eyes from the sizzling sun, and the warm breeze picked up bits of water from the boat's wake splashing them against his skin.

Ty became alive, unhinged, when he went out on his boat. He didn't care about social rules or proper behavior. He allowed the sun to toast his skin to a deep bronze, reminding him that he had a life outside Evans' Construction. His boat outings had two purposes. Fishing or hanging out with his buddies and having a couple of beers. This weekend was the latter and as he cruised down the river, he felt elation and freedom as air blasted through his hair.

No more Grace for the whole weekend.

They chose a spot in an area nicknamed Disappearing Island, which was just that: an island that disappeared during high tide. On weekends, people beached their boats around the perimeter of the sand bar and spent the day on the shore, drinking and partying until the tide washed away the island.

James enthusiastically jumped out of the hull as they approached the island and directed it onto the sandbar. There weren't many people yet, but Ty and James knew if they didn't get there early, they wouldn't get a spot. The couple next to them smiled as they eyed Ty's parking skills, relief washing over their faces when James finally shouted, "That's good, drop the anchor." Ty cut the engine, and then began passing items to James: chairs, coolers, a radio, portable grill, and some Frisbees.

Once they were settled, Ty took a seat in his red beach chair and leaned back as the sun coated his skin, closing his eyes to allow a wave of relief wash over him. He could hear James crack open a beer and asked for one. James handed his freshly opened beer to Ty before returning to the cooler for another.

Several boats approached and lined up around the island, relieving them of their solitude.

"God, it's a perfect day," James said, throwing himself into his own chair next to Ty. Ty closed his eyes again, wanting a moment of relaxation.

"Yeah, it is."

"Shit, look at this group of hotties." James smacked Ty's arm as a group of younger women cruised past them, giggling as they noticed James' attention.

"Dude, I'm done. After the shit Grace pulled last night, I'm done." Ty shook his head before resting it on the chair again, closing his eyes before he caught a glimpse of the girls.

"I know, right? That's some shit," James agreed.

"I'm done with women."

Ty opened his eyes when James didn't respond, curious about what distracted him. His eyes went to a beautiful brunette playing makeshift volleyball a few boats down from them.

A brunette he didn't want to see at the moment.

"Speak of the devil," James announced.

She looked amazing. Her hair cascaded down her back like a blanket and as she bounced with the ball, it waved, as if summoning him. Her simple black bikini hugged the curves of her butt perfectly, showing Ty exactly the shape her shorts had hidden the first day they met.

He sucked in a deep breath, unable to stop himself from staring. Her butt cheeks bounced with weightless abandon, and Ty lapped his tongue up like a sick dog.

Then he realized what he was doing and corrected himself immediately. Resolved to sit in his chair and bask in the sun, Ty closed his eyes and attempted to ignore her presence.

"I'll be right back," James declared.

"Where you going?"

"To say hi. I'll be back."

"Are you fucking crazy? I don't want her to know I'm here. She'll probably accuse me of following her."

"Grace!" James was making his way toward her before Ty finished speaking.

"Thanks, asshole."

Ty turned his chair so the sight of Grace was behind him. He lounged back further and closed his eyes again, refusing to turn around and see her reaction to his presence.

However, his hearing honed in on the conversation.

"You look hot," James was telling her.

The comment was received with a giggle. "Thanks. You don't look so bad yourself."

Ty rolled his eyes. Seriously? How old were they? Fifteen?

He silently begged James not to say he was there.

"Ty's here with me too. He's sitting down over there."

Ty cringed, hopefully not noticeably.

"Oh, really? Maybe I should go and say hello."

Ty settled deeper in his chair, sealing his eyes shut. He'd act like he was asleep. That was his spontaneous plan.

"Ty?"

He paused before opening his eyes then slowly opened them. He admired her for a split second. She had to know the effect she had on men.

"Grace." He couldn't hide the discontent in his voice.

"I didn't think this was your scene."

"If I had known it was yours, I wouldn't have come."

She didn't respond, just placed her hand on her very exposed hip. That damn hip!

Feeling awkward, Ty stood to reach for his shirt draped behind his chair. He didn't want to be accused of anything.

He felt her eyes on him like they were coated in glue. She was surveying him. She was checking him out.

He paused in gathering his shirt, reveling in his hotness for a moment, just to give himself something to use when she accused him of lusting after her.

"Are you checking me out?" he asked.

Grace blushed crimson.

"Absolutely not." She lifted her shoulders a little taller and met his eyes with a determined look.

"Interesting, because I could have sworn I just saw you staring," he teased. He decided to abandon his shirt and remain undressed for a moment longer.

"Why would I check you out?"

"I don't know. Maybe you accused me of wanting you because deep down you want me?" His voice was thick with seduction. The beer that pumped in his blood helped with his nerves.

Her cheeks turned deep red again, so she turned her attention to James.

"It was nice seeing you again, James. I'll call you later."

Then she strutted away. Ty and James both enjoyed the view of her backside until she disappeared behind the crowd ahead of them.

When Ty turned to James to ask what was going on between the two of them, he had walked away to gather another beer.

Ty let it go and settled back into his chair.

Two could play at that game.

BOYS WILL BE BOYS

*G*race fought everything in her body to not turn around, knowing damn well both guys were watching her ass as she walked away.

Ty was right, she was checking him out. Who wouldn't? He was Adonis in the flesh, with his bronze skin and thoroughly chiseled body. She couldn't help but appraise him. Just because he got under her skin and forced her to reevaluate every decision she ever made didn't mean that she couldn't be physically attracted to him.

Then she thought about the look on James' face when he caught her appraising Ty. He looked so lost and hurt. That made her feel guilty. She liked James and even found an attraction to him but when Ty was around she felt something altogether different. It was almost primal.

She continued to strut away, still fighting every urge she had to turn around, when her flock of girlfriends approached when she was within their invisible boundary, bombarding her with questions about the two hunks she had been talking to.

"It's just two guys I work with." She tried to justify their existence without much commotion. It was just Ty and James after all. They didn't deserve a grand introduction. At least not to her girls.

"Are you dating one of them?" Jamie always dug the deepest, like she was a novice reporter set out to make her mark.

"Hell no. Men are a pain in the ass."

"Is the dark haired one single?" Jaime asked.

"Ty? Yeah."

And just like that, she was able to pass them off to one of her girlfriends. All sorts of ideas began to swirl around her circle of friends as they speculated about the two men within yards of them.

Grace went back to the boat, escaping their endless questions and grabbed another blackberry and watermelon drink, determined to mask her discomfort with some good alcohol. Once she jumped down from the boat, she located an empty chair and sat down for the first time since she'd arrived on the beach. The balmy sun started to toast Grace, surrounding her so that she could succumb to the relaxation it offered. The sound of the waves lapping against the beach slowly disappeared as she coasted into a light sleep. Every so often, a loud or unsettling sound would bring her back to consciousness, but just enough to make her roll her eyes and return to her slumber. The tepid sun continued to warm her as Ty started to appear in her mind.

He was shirtless, strolling down the beach in her direction. Her friends had somehow disappeared and she looked frantically for someone to distract him from her, knowing all too well she wouldn't be strong enough for a man like Ty. When she glanced around her chair, she was the only person on the small island, all the boats and people gone, causing her to face Ty alone. Just as she opened her mouth to say something, Grace rose in embarrassment, gulping for air as if she had been drowning.

"Welcome back," Jamie teased as Grace bounded from her chair.

"I guess I didn't realize I had nodded off. How long was I out?"

"Couple of hours. I hope you had sunscreen on."

Thank God, she did.

Grace glanced towards Ty's boat to find that both men had left their chairs, their boat sitting unattended on the crowded beach. Their absence made her regret everything that had happened in the past twenty-four hours. Poor James clearly thought they were headed in a relationship direction and Ty thought she was attracted to him.

What was she going to do?

The sand island slowly disappeared with the sun and Grace started to gather her friends so they could leave before the high tide swept them under water. Having too much to drink herself, she was finding the task very difficult. Grace felt like a mother of six toddlers frantically trying to get them out of the house before she was late to work. Except one child didn't want to get up from her chair, one was too focused on a group of guys, one was on her phone arguing with someone, another was too busy finishing a sand castle and the last two had strayed into No Man's Land, talking to Ty and James.

Grace gathered all but the last two, depositing them onto the rented boat. Then she gave herself a pep talk, reminding herself she was just going over there to collect her two dimwitted friends.

She took a deep breath and headed out, preparing herself for what felt like an adventure of her lifetime. She was venturing into enemy territory.

"Speak of the devil," James commented when Grace stepped into their circle.

His face lit with a genuine smile.

"Why? What did I do?" Grace asked.

"I was just asking your lovely friends here if they wanted to come to my Halloween party."

James and his partying. Grace was beginning to see a theme.

"And? Did they accept the invite?"

"Of course, they did. And you and Ty are coming too," James announced.

Grace cringed at the sound of their names stuck together with the word 'and'.

"We'll see. Come on Ashley and Erica. We need to get going."

"Grace can give you two my number," James chimed after them as Grace slowly directed them back to their boat.

When Grace reached the boat, she helped each friend climb on, then placed it in reverse so she could back out and make her way back to the dock and safely back to her motel.

"So what's the deal with you and Ty?" James questioned her when she called him later that night. She had been snuggled in her bed watching an old episode of *Hell's Kitchen*.

"Ty? Nothing." She turned the volume down on the TV.

"Bullshit."

"Seriously. It's nothing," Grace insisted, tipping her head back into her pillow.

"Then why'd you accuse him of wanting to sleep with you?" James actually sounded jealous.

"He told you about that?" Grace was surprised that Ty had shared that, especially with James.

"Yeah. He's my best friend."

"So, did you tell him we kissed?" She twirled some hair in her fingers.

"No. Why would I?" The tone of James voice changed to defiant.

"Well, you're best friends, aren't you?"

"Well, I didn't. It's none of his business." James was getting annoyed, she could hear it in his voice. Was he jealous?

"Maybe you should. Then he might back off." She flipped the covers so her feet were uncovered.

"Why? Was he pushy?"

"Depends what you call pushy." Grace moved the phone to her other ear.

"Ty's not pushy. I don't think he has any interest in you." Well, that stung.

"Then why'd he invite me back to his house?"

"Knowing him, he felt bad and just wanted to make it up to you."

"Why couldn't he do it at the bar, or at work?" Grace felt she had a valid question.

"Ty's a private guy. He doesn't like doing those kinds of things in public."

"That makes sense." She couldn't debate that point.

"Can we not talk about him?"

"Fine." She started to flip through the channels on her TV.

"Want to come over?" He sounded bored.

"Tonight?" She looked down at her pajamas.

"Yeah."

"James, it's late. I'll take a raincheck."

"Oh. Okay." She could hear the hurt in his voice. What did he expect? They were out in the sun all day. She was tired.

"Maybe tomorrow," Grace suggested. She clicked off the TV.

"Okay."

"I'm going to let you go now. It's getting late and I'm beat. It was nice seeing you today." She let out a yawn.

"You too," James replied.

Grace hung up the phone feeling more confused about Ty than before she called James.

STICKS AND STONES

*T*y arrived at the construction site promptly at six a.m. on Monday morning. He was hungover from the weekend, yet refreshed. It was quiet and the site was calm, allowing him time to plan out his day without annoying distractions, like James bugging him about Grace.

He sipped his hot coffee and hoped she wouldn't arrive before everyone else, like she was prone to do, so he could plan out his day without her distracting him. Plus, he needed to gather his wits and his sex drive. His damn body had a mind of its own, and he needed to control it. Grace was bad news. He knew it but his body didn't.

However, as if he had a sign on his back that read, *torture me*, Grace's shiny red car pulled up.

"Shit," he moaned under his breath and placed the hot cup of coffee on the tailgate of his truck, steam floating from its mouth.

Thankfully, it was still dark outside, so he was able to step into the shadow of his truck and avoid her.

He watched as she placed one lean leg and then the other onto the ground and climbed out of her car. She wore her usual tattered skinny jeans and an Evans' Construction t-shirt. Her hair was pulled back into a ponytail, and she, too, carried a steaming cup of coffee.

She didn't notice him at first and James couldn't deny himself the pleasure of watching her as she brushed a stray hair out of her eyes. Then she straightened her t-shirt by pulling on the hem so it went taut over her breasts.

Annoyed, Ty turned around and forced himself to look in a different direction. But, as usual, Grace walked around the truck to face him.

Her face lit with a hesitant smile as she acknowledged him. Ty's lungs grew heavy and his body grew hot as apprehension wrapped around the two of them. She shuffled her feet, kicking at the gravel as they struggled to maintain a common, comfortable ground.

"Good morning," she said. She took two hesitant steps toward him. Her words were clearly forced. If she didn't want to be here, then why had she come so early?

"Good morning."

"Did you have a good weekend?"

What do you think? You were there, ruining the fun at Disappearing Island.

"Yes. You?"

"I did. I worked Saturday night and last night, but I got awesome tips."

"That's good."

"Yeah, it helps pay the bills." She smiled a little nervously.

"I bet."

He collected his cup of coffee and opened his mouth to talk about what happened on Saturday just as James pulled up in his rusty, old, pickup truck. Ty decided against it and waited for James to get out, then said, "Good morning. Concrete's coming at noon."

"Good. So, I'll finish with the guys over there." James

73

pointed to the remaining sidewalk at the back of the site. With that comment, Ty's conversation with Grace was ended and she followed James to the sidewalk. Ty watched the two of them as they walked side by side. They didn't touch each other, but it was obvious to him that something was happening between the two of them. Her eyes held a smile and his body language hinted that he was attracted to her. Ty just shook his head and turned his attention back to the plans on his truck.

More men arrived, which allowed Ty to suspend any thoughts about Grace and James as he delegated tasks and set the construction site in motion.

"James, I need you and the concrete guys to focus on the pour over here," Ty directed an hour later, his phone pressed to his ear as Mr. Evans explained a Change Order.

The guys were working in full swing at that point, and the construction machine was well underway. It was going to be a smooth day, where everything worked in sync.

"John, the trusses are coming at eleven. Make sure everything is in order and this area is clear." He continued making his rounds while dictating tasks. He got lost in the hectic hustle of a busy day: answering phone calls, directing shipments, managing his men, losing track of time.

It wasn't until he dismissed the men at the end of the day that he realized Grace was nowhere in sight.

Had she left? No way. She wouldn't leave without telling someone.

A small bubble of panic weighed on his chest as he surveyed the job.

She wasn't at the water's edge or by the restroom building.

Her fire hydrant colored car was still parked at the construction gate, so she was somewhere close by.

James approached him, noticing Ty's hint of alarm.

"What's wrong?"

"Nothing. Why?" Ty snapped.

"Bullshit. Are the trusses on right?"

"Yeah, everything's fine," Ty lowered his voice and hoped James would get the hint and do the same. "I just don't see Grace."

"Oh. She's probably in the shitter."

"No, I checked."

"Maybe she left without saying goodbye." James nudged Ty with his shoulder.

"No, her car's here."

James shrugged and indicated that he had no clue but wasn't worried and turned his attention back to bringing tools to his truck.

Ty peeked around the side of the job trailer. Maybe she was changing her clothes. He had made her work in the water today.

She was there, and thankfully, she wasn't changing but instead was leaning against the job trailer. She didn't notice him at first, because she was focused on what she was doing. Her left leg was propped against the trailer to support the weight of her small frame. She had her right pant leg rolled up to her knee and was bending over to apply some water from a bottle to her shin.

"Fuck," she hissed under her breath. She sucked in some air through her teeth as the water collided with a large gash down the front of her shin and bright red blood poured down her leg, staining the top of her white sock.

"Shit, Grace," Ty scolded, rushing to her when he realized what was going on.

She looked up at the sound of his voice; her eyes wide with panic.

"Ty." Her voice was one of shock and fear. That's when Ty realized she was trying to hide the gash on her leg.

Why?

Then he realized he now had a reason to remove her from the job site and possibly Evans' Construction entirely, a work injury and Workman's Comp.

GIVING UP THE FIGHT

*G*race looked up, her eyes beseeching him.

"It's not that bad."

"Not that bad! Are you kidding me? This," he lifted his shirt and exposed his side, pointing to a scar, "was not that bad and it required two stitches. You need to go to the hospital."

"I'm fine."

"You're not fine."

She looked down at her shin. Blood continued to pour from the wound, forcing her to realize it was as bad as it looked. But she refused to admit it. Instead, she delegated tasks that needed her attention.

"I need a rag or something."

"Here." Before she could reject, he removed his shirt and placed it over her shin, the material immediately absorbing her blood.

"Thanks. Can you ask James if he could drive me home?"

"I can drive you."

"I'd prefer you didn't."

"Fine. James!" His voice was so loud, Grace flinched as it pierced her ears.

As if James had been eavesdropping, he appeared, took one look at her leg and offered his assistance.

"Can you bring her home?" Ty asked, or rather demanded.

"Yeah."

"I'm going to call her dad."

"Oh no you're not. My father doesn't need to know a thing about this. I'll get home, shower and bandage myself up and tomorrow no one will know what happened."

"Grace, I have to report this to him."

"You don't have to report a damn thing."

"You need stiches."

"What? Are you a doctor now? I told you I've got this. If James can just drive me home."

Grace saw the exchange between both men. The unspoken Bro Code.

Then James picked her up and carried her bridal style to his truck. She noticed his strength as he carried her with ease. James wasn't as muscular as Ty, yet his body deceived her. She felt a tingle of appreciation for this newly discovered trait.

He placed her in the truck and she noticed the inside left much to be desired. The old cloth seats were tattered, turning black in some areas where years of wear had worn them down to exposed fibers. It smelled like a stale cigarette and grease. Grace tried not to judge the filth, knowing it was mostly due to the historical aspect of the truck and not to James' hygiene rituals.

He climbed into the driver's side and rolled down his window to let a fresh breeze fill the cab, which allowed some of the stale cigarette to leave. Ty followed them to the truck giving directions as to what they should be doing.

Ty reminded her of Ben in so many ways. The way he walked into an incident and immediately took charge, ensuring she was taken care of. It was one trait she had appreciated in Ben.

"I've got this. I know what needs to be done," Grace told both of them.

"I know you do," Ty said.

Then James nodded his head to Ty, tipping his baseball cap and drove off before Grace could say another word.

"He's expecting me to bring you to the hospital."

"I know. And I know you're going to respect when I ask you not to."

"Why not?" James questioned.

"Because I can't afford it, for one, and I don't need my dad finding out."

"You know you don't have to worry about the money."

"Really? And live with my dad reminding me a second time that I have failed. No thank you."

"Grace."

"James." She fixed a stare on him, almost rolling her eyes.

"Fine. I'll bring you to the motel."

When she was finally settled in her room, after having taken a shower and bandaging her shin, James left. He was polite and only offered his help in the most chivalrous way.

Only shortly after there was a light knock on her door. She assumed James had forgotten something.

"Who is it?"

"It's Dad."

Shit.

"It's open," she called from her spot on the bed.

The door squeaked when he opened it, wide enough to allow his XL body to fit through.

"I know what you're thinking." She tried to stand when he approached the bed, only to sit back down when she met pain.

"Do you now?"

"I'm fine," Grace insisted.

"No, you're not. Now, let me see it."

"Dad, seriously. I'm fine."

"Grace, let me see it," he growled.

Defeated, she unwillingly unwrapped her leg and allowed her father to inspect it.

"Come on. We're going to the hospital. You need stitches."

"No, I don't. I'm fine."

"I'm not going to argue with you. Let's go. I can still carry you, you know."

"No, you can't. Don't be silly," Grace tried again.

"Let's go. Now."

"Fine. Just give me a few moments to get dressed."

She'd stall as long as she could. That was the plan.

"No. Now. You're dressed. Let's go." He was on to her plan, obviously. He took her by the hand and guided her out the door to his SUV. She hobbled behind him, unable to move too fast as the throbbing started.

"Dad, come on. Seriously. I don't need to go to the hospital."

"Grace! Do you remember what happened the last time you told me you were fine and refused to go to the hospital?"

"That's not fair. This is different," Grace replied.

"Is it? Because I remember a very similar scenario. I remember every second of that day. Every word. Every detail. Everything I learned about that man and what he did to you."

"Dad, that's different."

"Really? Because all I see is my daughter needing help and refusing it because of her damn pride. Now please, let's go."

She didn't have it in her. She couldn't fight him any longer. He was right, she needed his help and it was about time she took it.

UNOFFICIAL DATE

*I*t was Thursday now, and the morale at the site had declined drastically each day because Grace wasn't present. The guys grew somber and worked alongside each other silently. No one spoke and no one questioned what happened to Grace, which indicated to Ty that rumors had spread like a virus but no one would step forward and ask what really happened. They worked with a rhythm, without motivation or ambition. Ty didn't realize the effect she had on everyone until she was gone.

"Do you think she'll come back?" James asked Ty as they sat at the water's edge eating lunch. It was a warmer day and as they sat at the edge of the dock, feet dangling over the edge, a boat cruised down the river, leaving a wake that would surely disrupt the turbidity barrier.

"I have no clue. Bill said the doctor won't allow her to walk on it for at least two weeks."

"That sucks. This whole thing sucks." James stuffed his face with cold pizza that had been wrapped in aluminum foil in his ratty lunch bag.

"Have you gone to see her?" Ty asked.

"Yeah. I've brought her dinner a couple of times. You?"

"You have? I didn't know that," Ty paused mid-bite to gaze upon his friend. A bubble of heat rose in his throat as he contemplated James and Grace together. He thought for a moment longer then returned to his sandwich.

"Yeah."

"I never even thought about checking on her," Ty remarked.

"Yeah, I know. She told me."

"She told you? Really?"

"She told me last night."

"Just how many times have you been there?" Ty asked.

"I don't know. Three or four?"

Shit. Ty was usually that guy, the father of the group who always ensured everyone was okay. When James had fallen once and broken his ankle, Ty was at his house every night checking on him. He hadn't even considered checking on her.

Damn James! Now he'd have to go and check on her even if only to save face. He was her boss, in a way. He should have checked on her already.

"Just how close are the two of you?"

"Grace and I?"

"Yeah."

"We've gone on a few dates. Kissed."

"No shit. I didn't know that."

"But I don't think she's that into me. She keeps bringing up her ex... Ben, I think his name was."

"Is that so?"

"Yeah. I tried though."

"I guess you did."

Ty wrapped up the remainder of his sandwich and returned it to his lunch bag, then gave the signal that lunch was over, returning everyone to their assignments for the day.

∿

LATER THAT NIGHT he pulled into the run-down motel with fresh Chinese takeout in his passenger seat. His truck was filled with the smell of pork fried rice and sweet and sour chicken.

God this place was awful, Ty thought to himself as he scoped out the parking, looking for her bright red yoyo. He found it parked in front of one of the units wedged in-between a beat-up older sedan and an outdated minivan.

He pulled his truck into the spot next to the minivan and prayed he had chosen the right door. James had told him Unit 4, but James wasn't always reliable with facts.

Lifting his hand to knock on the door, Ty paused.

What the hell was he doing? The last time they were alone together she accused him of lusting after her.

With an exhale, he decided it was too late to turn back now. His loud knock resonated off the walls of the hotel room and echoed back to Ty at the door.

"Dad! I don't need anything," Grace's annoyed voice called in response.

"It's not your dad. It's me, Ty."

There was silence for a moment then she opened the door, the frame shook as it unstuck from the door.

"What do you want?" she asked.

Ty studied her for a moment. She looked like a wildflower —no makeup, red high heels, or tight jeans. Her hair was pulled up in a loose bun, with her body in a loose t-shirt, and a thin pair of jean shorts.

"I brought Chinese," he smiled, curling the bag up so she could see the proof.

"Why?"

"Just being nice," he smiled, hoping she wouldn't leave him out there like an idiot.

"Why?"

Okay, so maybe she was going to make him stay outside like an idiot.

83

"Just because," he told her, shifting his weight and tilting his head to plead with her to let him in. She studied him for a moment, her fuzzy slippers padding on the floor when she finally backed away, leaving the door open for him to enter.

The room smelled fresh and clean even though it was a small, standard motel room. The king-sized bed was made, and everything appeared to be put away.

There were plug-ins pumping out a clean linen scent from outlets around the room. Ty closed the door behind himself, peaking outside for one last surveillance of the parking lot before locking it.

"It's not as glorious as your place." She stepped away from him, her weight on one hip with her arms crossed at her chest, waiting for what he didn't know.

"It's not bad."

"Really?" She tried to hide the sarcasm as she looked down at the floor, slightly bending at the hip, preoccupying herself with a stain on the carpet.

"Why aren't you staying at your dad's?" Ty asked as he placed the food on the small round table by the front window.

"Why do you care?"

"I don't. Just trying to make conversation," Ty answered, turning his attention to her.

"You know why."

"So, you're living here to prove a point?" Ty confirmed.

"Well, when you say it like that."

"Look, I get it. You want people to realize that you're not some brat."

"Exactly."

"How's your leg?"

"It's fine. I think my dad overreacted. He keeps bugging me to come home."

"Well, you did get thirteen stitches. Maybe you should go home."

"Nope. I can do this on my own."

"You know, it's okay to admit that you can't handle some things." Ty pulled the Styrofoam takeout containers out of the brown paper bag.

"Like you should admit you're attracted to me?"

Ty stopped short and looked at her. Her pristine eyes held a sensual light.

"Maybe you should admit you're attracted to me," Ty retorted.

She rolled her eyes but couldn't hide the pink from staining her cheeks.

"So, you admit it!" He pointed in her direction with a teasing smile on his lips.

"I admit nothing," she responded and motioned for him to join her at the table and eat.

"You don't have to. I can see it in your eyes," he teased.

"Seriously? I don't feel an attraction toward you."

"Keep telling yourself that." Ty took a seat and opened the to-go container in front of him. "So, on another note, James told me to remind you his Halloween party is in two weeks." Ty placed the open container in front of her.

"Yeah, he keeps telling me. I haven't decided if I'm going."

"Why not? It's the event of the year." Ty tried to remain unaffected as her over-stretched t-shirt slid down her right shoulder.

Her creamy white shoulder.

"Do *you* want me to go?" She smiled coyly without placing her shirt back on her shoulder.

"I don't care what you do. I'm just relaying James' message."

Why didn't he see a bra strap on her shoulder? Her whole shoulder was exposed, and he didn't see the damn strap, which meant one thing.

"Do you want me to go with you? Do you not have a date?"

He heard her, but he couldn't concentrate because of her bare shoulder.

"I'm sorry, what did you say?" Shit, she had said something, but he didn't hear it.

"I asked if you had a date."

"No. You can go if you want. I was just reminding you, that's all." He briefly closed his eyes to try to compose himself.

Lift your sleeve. Oh God, please.

"Okay then, it's a date. You can pick me up at seven." She smiled with her seductive eyes.

Holy shit. What just happened?

LEAVE

*G*race closed the door behind Ty and leaned against it in exhaustion. She could hear him unlock his truck, climb in and bring it to life before backing out of the parking spot and leaving her behind, only to hear a clearly intoxicated couple yelling at each other moments later.

What had she just done?

She thumped her head against the door and chastised herself for being so impulsive with her words—hell, with every decision in her life.

What the hell was wrong with her? Why did she initiate a date with him? He clearly didn't want a date with her. Then there was James. She shoved herself away from the door and checked the curtains to make sure they were covering the window completely. She then stared at the vacant food containers on her small table and shook her head. Maybe he did want a date but didn't know how to ask.

She was doomed.

FOR THE NEXT week or so, as the doctor had directed, she remained off her feet, allowing the gash on her leg to heal. She struggled with cabin fever and relished the unscheduled visits from her father and a few of her friends. It broke the monotonous silence she dealt with each day.

She found herself wondering if Ty would stop by again after his last unexpected visit.

Actually, it became more than wondering. She started to look forward to it, hope for it, and even crave it.

However, over a week of solitude passed by, and she didn't hear a word from him. Her mood became somber, and she felt herself slip into disappointment as cabin fever raged. She assumed he was caught in the working web of construction and didn't have time to stop by and visit with her.

She needed to get out. She was sitting in her rank hotel room, waiting for his appearance like a love struck teenage girl. It was sickening.

She tried to study her textbooks from college, keeping herself apprised of the latest information so she didn't feel dimwitted on the site. She wasn't going to let this little setback stop her from proving to her father she could run the business.

Finally, after two painful weeks, she crossed the finish line as she left the doctor's office. She was given the okay to return to her normal activities. It had been a stupid mistake that would place a scar on her leg, reminding her like a tattoo that she needed to be on point at all times. This was a lesson. She needed to treat it as such and move forward.

She quickly called her father and reported the news.

"So, you're clear to return to work?"

"Yes, Dad. I'm on my way to the job site now. See? Even when I fall I can get back up and handle my own."

She could hear her father exhale his disappointment.

"Grace, I don't want you out there."

"Too late, Dad. I'm here," she explained and then hung up

the phone as she pulled her petite car onto the site. Freedom at last.

A lot had happened since she was last there. The building was almost complete, and the subcontractors were working diligently to install pole lights that would line the tree-canopied park.

She didn't immediately spot Ty, but assumed he was somewhere around the site. She'd come to realize, after sitting alone for two weeks, that Ty was a workaholic. He was also a damn good superintendent, who really made jobs run smoothly. She was mad at first when he reported her injury but after contemplating on it for some time, she realized he'd done the best thing he could have done. He protected her.

She took in a rejuvenating breath and took her time climbing out of the car, careful not to place too much weight on her recently released leg.

James was the first to spot her, and he came running from the other side of the site with a white-toothed grin.

"You're back!"

Grace smiled. "I am."

"Just in time, my party's next Saturday," James reminded her.

"Party?"

"Yeah, you know, my Halloween party. You told Ty you'd come." He frowned.

"Oh, yeah. I almost forgot. See? It's good I stopped by."

It was the party Ty had agreed to take her to—or rather, the party she had forced Ty to say he would take her to.

She had forgotten about that final conversation with him. Well, not entirely forgotten. She'd just forgotten about the date arrangement.

"Yeah. A lot has changed since you've been gone," James continued. Grace tried to focus on his words but felt foggy as her senses struggled to find Ty. Where was he? The site was bustling with activity, so he had to be around somewhere.

"I see the buildings pretty much done," she tried to add to the conversation.

"They finished that a couple of days ago," James explained. She could feel his intense gaze on her, as her eyes continued to scan the site for Ty.

"Ty's also gone," James blurted out as if he had been holding the bubble of truth in his mouth for weeks.

"You mean he took the day off?"

"No. He's gone. He had to take a personal leave. No one knows why."

Grace's heart dropped.

"When did he leave?"

"About a week ago."

No, he wasn't that weak of a man. He wouldn't cower because of her. Would he?

"So, who's running the site?"

"I am," James boasted, puffing his chest with pride.

"Good. That's good. I've gotta go. I need to have a chat with my dad."

"Oh, okay." James held his hands up in surrender and backed away as Grace retreated back to her car.

SPEAK NOW OR FOREVER HOLD YOUR PEACE

ngagement Notice:
Stephanie Writer and Justin Benson, together with their parents, would like to announce their wedding engagement. Stephanie Writer, a native of Daytona Beach, said yes on Sunday evening after Justin Benson, formerly from Washington State, proposed. The wedding is scheduled for March, 2016.

TY RE-READ the notice in the newspaper several times the morning after his promising dinner with Grace, allowing the words to dissolve like a poison into his heart.

Engagement.

Five years of busting his ass, of proving himself and rising to the top, and it was all for nothing. She had moved on. She had gotten engaged.

Engaged!

He crumpled the newspaper in his fist and angrily threw it in the trash.

"Ty, I'm sorry. But I think you need to grow up and become

a man before you want to become my husband," she had said and left him on bended knee in the middle of the restaurant.

So, he had done just that. He grew up, using the three-thousand dollar check she mailed him for his half of the belongings he left behind in their apartment and invested it in the purchase of a house. His house. The house he had just finished.

For her.

Ty couldn't place his anger. He feared it would hurt no matter where he placed it in his heart.

She had gotten engaged to someone else.

"Agh!" He screamed at the top of his lungs, thrusting his hands through his hair and then slamming his fists on his cold countertop.

He had to do something. He couldn't just allow her to cast him aside and move on with her life, not after everything he had done for her.

So, he decided he'd head to Stephanie's.

~

BILL EVANS DIDN'T HIDE his shock when Ty asked for the sudden personal leave. He didn't hide his annoyance either. Ty requested the time off without an explanation and explained to Bill that he would be home in a week's time.

As promised, Ty returned to the job site on Monday morning. He felt resentful, angry, and let down, but at the same time he felt relieved and prepared to move on.

Stephanie had been apologetic. She held him, cried with him, and eventually prompted him to go home and accept that she had moved on.

"Ty, we weren't going to work," she had told him. "You've changed; you're right. You did everything I asked. But I don't love you anymore. Do you really want to be with someone who doesn't love you?"

Ty's heart felt like a bee had stung him, and it pounded with a relentless ache. But in the end, she was right. He couldn't be with someone who didn't love him.

He deserved more.

No one knew what to expect when he returned to the job site on Monday morning. Everyone danced around him, as if he would pounce on any of them at any given moment and he didn't make an effort to ease their discomfort either. James was the first to approach and Ty inwardly cursed him for being, well, James.

"Where have you been?"

"I had some personal matters to attend to," Ty grumbled as he eyed his dock contractor, who was using his pile driving equipment on a barge he really didn't trust. He held back a raging fire of emotions.

"And what did it pertain to?"

Ty gave James a warning glance, exhaling his annoyance.

"Just wanted to make sure you're okay." James held his hands up in surrender.

"I'm fine."

"Grace came back on Friday. She looked great."

"Is that so?"

"Yeah, her leg looked really good. I guess she's in the office with her dad this week."

Ty snorted under his breath and rolled his eyes. Good. He couldn't face her right now

"She's worried about you," James added.

"Well, she doesn't need to be," Ty grumbled and turned to bark at one of the workers. He needed to calm down. James was just trying to help.

"What the hell happened to you?" James implored, slightly shoving Ty back so he was in front of him. Ty looked at him and swelled in anger.

"Back off."

James planted his feet. "No. What the hell happened?"

Something inside Ty exploded and a surge of pent up anger pushed him to shove James to the side. James staggered a moment, disbelief etched on his face but he didn't waver.

"I warned you," Ty told James, as he pulled his powerful arm back and punched James in the rib cage. James took the blow, bending at the waist but stood back up and shoved Ty with his shoulder, sending him to the dusty ground.

"What the fuck is your problem?" James demanded, rocking back and forth.

Ty remained on the ground, making no attempt to stand.

"I told you to back off!"

A crowd was gathering around them now.

"What the hell happened to you?" James demanded again.

"That's none of your business." Ty stood in one fluid motion.

"It may be none of his business, but it is mine." The crowd parted as Grace stepped into the circle. She was dressed in starched, black, dress pants and a casual blouse, showcasing her narrow waist.

Ty shook his head violently, then shouted, "It's fine! Everyone get back to work!"

His entire backside was covered with dust and dirt, and Grace reached out to brush the debris from him. Ty jumped at the touch of her petite hands on his back. He felt electrified for a moment, as the casual gesture sent heat throughout his body.

He turned to face her, her face innocent and full of concern. Her vibrant blue eyes begged him to calm down and come back to an even temper. His breathing had become labored, and Ty struggled to get his emotions in check.

"James, can you take over? Ty and I need to have a talk." Grace looked over at him.

James nodded.

"This isn't over," James warned Ty before painfully walking away. Regret started to invade Ty.

Grace dragged his attention back to her when she wrapped her fingers around his thick forearm.

"Come with me," she told him, pulling him toward her car, igniting a sexual sensation deep in Ty's gut.

He resisted and she pulled him with more force and a look of determination.

"You either get in my car now or start looking for another job," she ordered.

Ty reluctantly climbed into Grace's car and buckled his seat belt. He reached under the seat and adjusted it to allow himself more room.

Grace took her seat in one fluid motion. Her legs had ample space as her feet found their home on the pedals. She didn't speak as they drove away from the job site.

"Where are we going?" Ty didn't hide the impatience in his voice. He didn't care that she flinched a little at his bark; neither did he care where they were going.

"Lunch. So we can talk. I hope food can help you find your way back to decency." Her voice was crisp. She didn't take her attention from the road as they made their way to whatever restaurant she had in mind.

"I'm fine."

"Really?"

"Look. I don't need to talk. What I need is to get back to work." He moved in an attempt to divert her attention, but she didn't waver and kept her sight on the road.

She paused for a moment, clearly thinking out her response.

"Back to work? Picking a fight with James isn't work." Grace finally took her attention from the road to glare at him.

"I told him to back off."

"Well, we're not backing off until we know what the hell happened while you were gone."

"It's none of your business."

"It became my business when you started throwing punches at James."

She turned into a gravel parking lot of a local fishing shack, which ended the conversation. Deck Down Under was a small restaurant on the river. It served fresh fish caught right off of their own dock. Ty hadn't been there in years because it was Stephanie's favorite place—well, it used to be until she moved out of state.

Grace parked the car and climbed out, not waiting for Ty. She was approaching the entrance when Ty finally climb out of the car.

"Two please, over by the water." Grace smiled at the hostess, who grabbed two aged laminated menus and directed them to a small white plastic table in the far corner of the outdoor restaurant. Their table was on the edge of the dock and schools of fish could be seen in the murky water.

Grace seated herself first and Ty took the seat opposite her, diverting his attention over the wooden railing to the cloudy water below. He was hesitant to sit back in his seat for fear that the plastic chair would buckle under his weight.

"Now, we're going to order, and then you're going to tell me what the hell happened," she dictated while studying the sticky menu.

Ty just nodded, his eyes still fixated on the water below, hoping a fish would jump.

They both ordered when the overzealous server attended to them. Ty studied the young server, returning her smiles with his own.

"Thank you. That'll be all." Grace interrupted the vixen's flirting so they could get to business.

The server gave her a nervous smile, glanced at Ty once more and left.

"So, I doubt you will voluntarily give up the information I want. But know this: if you don't tell me and let me help you sort it out, you will lose your job."

Her eyes bore into him like laser rays melting into a wall.

"It's none of your business. I'm fine. I'll apologize to James when we return, and there won't be another issue."

"It is my business if you are picking fights at the job."

Who made her the boss all of a sudden?

"I told you it won't happen again."

"It better not."

He sat back in his seat and crossed his arms over his chest like a toddler who had just lost his candy. Ty could almost hear the sound of her whip in the background.

"Look, Ty. I know you don't like when people pry in your personal business, but maybe we can help."

Ty smirked and shook his head.

"Unless you can make my ex call off her engagement, you can't help me," he said, then returned his arms to his chest, as if the action would protect his heart from the sudden ache assaulting it.

"So, it was her?" Grace's face flooded with concern, and she reached her hands across the table.

Ty stared at them, noticing her bright red fingernails and the lack of jewelry. He dreamed for a split second that those hands were consoling him in another way, a purely sexual no-relationship-attached kind of way.

"She moved on, didn't she?" Her voice seemed distant, and the sympathy dripping from her words stung Ty like acid.

"Yes, she did. So, let's change the fucking subject!"

"Okay, I understand. We'll leave it alone." She retracted her cold hands. "You know James' party is Saturday night, right?"

Ty lounged back into his seat, silently praying it didn't buckle and took in a deep breath. They sat in silence for a few moments as chaotic thoughts blew around in his head. Grace attempted to revive the conversation several times, only to fail. What could he say to her? How could he explain the implosive feelings he was bearing on his own? Thankfully, the server returned with their food and placed each plate on the table with a hesitant smile allowing both of them a distraction. Grace politely accepted the food and urged the waitress to leave them again.

"You're right. The party totally skipped my mind," Ty finally answered, almost forgetting that she had mentioned it before.

"I figured. I think you might need to make amends with James before Saturday. It might be a good time to show you've straightened things out." She took well-mannered bites of her food.

Shit. I'm supposed to be her date for the party.

"Look, I think it's best we go alone," he clarified, taking a bite of food as an excuse not to further explain why.

Women suck, that's why.

He watched a look of shock, hurt, annoyance, and pain flash across Grace's guarded eyes, then she presented him with a smile.

Her answer was awkward and painful to watch. Ty gawked as she painfully swallowed her food, chasing it with some water, then gulped some air before finally answering.

"That's fine."

CHOICES

For the first time since Grace returned home from college, her facade crumbled a little on the edges. Ty's rejection actually hurt. She didn't want to admit it, but it did, a lot. But as she met his eyes from across the table, she tucked that hurt deep away and focused on what needed to happen next.

"When we get back, I'll manage the job while you and James work things out."

"I don't need to 'work things out' with James. He gets it."

"You sure?"

He rolled his eyes. He was so hard to read. Grace didn't know if he was being rude or just himself.

"Yes, I'm sure. Now, are you done? I'd like to get back."

She looked down at her full plate then back up at him.

"I just started."

"Well, hurry up. I want to get back."

She took a of couple hasty bites then succumbed to his impatience and requested a box to go. There wasn't much more she could do.

She thought something was growing between the two of them but clearly she was wrong.

The waitress placed the check on the table between them.

Ty's hand brushed Grace's creating a jolt as he reached for the check.

"Ty, I've got it," she said, squirming a little at the influx of heat the small contact created.

Why was she reacting to him? He didn't show an interest in her.

"Now, what kind of man allows a lady to pay for his meal? I may be an asshole, but I do have manners," he warned her and snatched the check from her hands.

There was a sliver of flirtation in his eye and a hint of a smile on his lips as Grace honorably allowed him to fulfill his duty.

Maybe there was hope after all.

THE FOLLOWING NIGHT, Grace stood in front of the floor length mirror in her motel room, strutting uncomfortably like a model.

What was she thinking? A skin-tight Wonder Woman body suit? Really?

She wondered what Ty would think. Would he roll his mahogany eyes at her and walk away? Or would that little light, that speck of flirtation, bubble its way up as he saw her as a woman, not a threat?

There was only one way to find out.

An hour later, she knocked on the faded red front door of James' modest, but dated, beach bungalow. She held a bottle of Grey Goose in her left hand and her purse in the other. From the sounds of the vibrating walls, booming rap music, and cars wrapped around the block, the party seemed to be in full swing.

She debated whether she should leave and send her regrets via text as she waited for someone to answer the door. Ty was going to roll his eyes; she knew it.

Before the angel on her left shoulder could win, James quickly swung the front door open. His body was swaying from alcohol as his face lit with an over-expressive smile. He stumbled forward to embrace Grace in an awkward hug.

"Holy shit, you made it. You look, wow." He smiled, stepping aside so she could walk into the house. Grace felt his eyes survey every inch of her exposed body and she regretted her choice of outfit even more.

She liked James but the more time they spent together the more she realized he wasn't interested in her, just her body.

The small living room was packed. People mingled in every corner of the room, occupying couches, end tables and open floor space. She didn't think James knew as many people as he had crammed into his small house.

Interrupting her appraisal of his home, James placed his hand on the small of her back and whispered in her ear, "I can't believe you wore something sexy. It's so hot," while placing his body too close to her and making her uncomfortable.

"Thanks," she answered with a wearisome smile.

"Wow, I'm glad I'm single," he jested and brought her further into the house. "You want something to drink?" he asked her, politely collecting the Grey Goose from her hand and depositing it on a table with the other liquor.

Grace gazed around the room looking for someone, anyone, she knew. There were many people there; some dressed in Halloween costumes but most in casual clothes. As regret over her outfit continued to sink in; she sought out anyone who would make the situation a little more comfortable.

"Nah, I'm fine." She was trying to keep the contents in her stomach intact.

"Are you sure?" James brushed some of her hair behind her shoulder.

"Yeah, I'm sure."

"God, you're a hot superhero."

"How much have you had to drink?" she asked, attempting to step away.

"A lot!" He smiled and swayed back into her. "You wanna see the house?"

"You've got so many people crammed in here; it would be difficult to show me anything. Maybe another time?"

"Aww, you sure? I could show you my bedroom,"

Shit.

SAVING THE SUPERHERO

On the other side of the house, Ty stood in the kitchen sucking down three shots of tequila with the hope no one else would notice his raging nerves.

Where the hell was Grace?

Even though he had told her that he wanted to go to the party alone, he didn't want to be alone. When they had left the fish shack yesterday, he regretted placing distance between the two of them. She had been quiet and awkward the rest of the day.

He really wanted to try and make things up to her. He was an asshole. There was no other way around it. He was angry that Stephanie gave up on him, and he realized that she had sentenced him to a future of being alone.

He shot back another shot. The warm alcohol slid down his throat and warmed his gut.

When Grace stepped into the kitchen, oblivious that he was there, it was as if everything stopped. The music faded, the crowds of people parted, and all Ty could see was a full-body spandex suit glued to her amazingly fit body.

His breath caught in his throat, and all of his manners flew out the window. Every inappropriate, demeaning, sexual fantasy that could have crossed his mind did in that moment. And the alcohol didn't help.

Shit. He wanted to be polite. He wanted to leave an impression.

He wanted to leave the prison Stephanie had sentenced him to.

He didn't want to be alone.

He watched in slow motion, as James placed his greedy hand on the small of Grace's back and whispered something in her ear. Ty knew how James got when he was drunk. He had been witness to it too many times. He would home in on one woman and latch on until his sexual appetite was satisfied, sometimes pushing the limits of appropriate behavior.

A hint of panic flashed across Grace's eyes and Ty immediately sprang into action.

"Don't hit him. Don't hit him," Ty chanted to himself as he approached the two of them, attempting to look casual. "Grace! You made it," he announced as he swayed momentarily before finishing his trek across the room to her side.

Grace looked stunned as his body awkwardly stumbled into hers for a hug. He sucked in the scent of her freshly shampooed hair.

"Mmm. Your hair smells amazing," he spoke as the beer and whiskey slowed down his speech.

She pulled away from him and looked at him through hooded eyes.

"Ty, you're drunk," she spoke under her breath.

"Don't worry. I'll be fine."

"He's fine," James said, dismissing Ty with a brotherly shove. "We just need to get him drunk then laid."

"Grace, can we talk?" Ty asked, ignoring James' juvenile comment. He was a good friend, but he could be a pig when it came to women. He stretched a smile from ear to ear, sloppily attempting to appear sober.

"How much have you had to drink?" she asked under her breath, pulling him by the arm toward the back corner of the room along the grungy cabinets.

"Does it matter? I feel great."

"Ty…" She started to speak, but he cut her off completely driven by too much alcohol. He leaned over and gave in to his most carnal need, pressing his lips against hers as if it would be the last thing he'd do before dying right there in the middle of James' outdated kitchen.

Ty had no clue how she would respond. He half-expected to be slapped across the face and half-expected her to kiss him back, but in that moment, he didn't care. It felt so good to give in and allow himself to indulge for just a short moment.

She didn't pull away. Instead, her lips danced with his, and her tongue explored his. She didn't bring her arms up to embrace him, so he cradled her face in his large hands, directing her deeper into the breathtaking kiss.

The whole room went silent, and this time it wasn't Ty's imagination. Sudden intakes of breath were followed by amazed murmurs. The murmurs escalated to hushed conversations, and then backs were turned when the crowd realized that they weren't going to break the amazing connection that sparked between them.

Her lips were as soft as satin and as gentle as a kitten's touch. Her kiss held an ancient rhythm that both of their bodies innately knew how to respond to.

Feeling heat rise within his caged body, Ty hungrily pushed her into the dark laundry room off the kitchen. A raw need throbbed throughout his whole being, and his mouth sought to deepen the smoldering desire. He needed to extend the connection between their two bodies. Thousands of overwhelming emotions engulfed Ty, and he became frenzied with a burning ache. His cradling hands ran themselves through her hair and tipped her chin up for access to her neck.

"Ty," she whispered against his careless lips. Her voice held a hint of alarm, and he brought his eyes to hers.

"Ty," she whispered again, slowly pulling away.

Her departure broke Ty's spell, and like a hot cup of coffee the morning after, he realized the position he had placed both of them in. He backed away from her and ran his hands through his hair. Then he started pacing, turning to open the laundry room door to allow her to leave.

Shit. Shit. Shit.

"Ty! Grace!" James' voice cut through the curtain of heat they had created around themselves as he joined the two of them in the laundry room. "Come on. We're going to vote on best costume," he explained with a knowing smile spread across his face.

Ty looked at Grace, hoping a cloud of regret wasn't cast over her beautiful blue eyes.

Shit. Why couldn't he just remain sober? Just go into the kiss naturally instead of in a drunken stupor?

And why did James have to interrupt them?

Damn you, James.

CLAIM

*G*race had pulled herself out of Ty's embrace while both men stood there, dumbfounded and unable to react.

"I'm sorry," Ty finally croaked, clearing his throat. She could tell he regretted the ardent kiss the moment she broke the connection.

She wanted to scream at him and drill him with questions but he was drunk and couldn't really explain his behavior. Plus, did his actions indicate his true feelings? She would never know. Then there was James, who was too drunk to process what had happened. Both men were lust thirsty and she was the prey.

"Guys!" James prodded again, looking at the two of them as if the kiss hadn't even taken place.

"We're coming," Ty grumbled, answering for the two of them. Grace looked up as he brought his deep brown eyes down to her, the flame still burning deep in them. Grace tried to understand what he was thinking, but James continued to tug him away.

She opened her mouth to speak but he finally backed away,

breaking their gaze. He sauntered off, shaking James' hand from his arm. He never looked back, leaving her stunned and alone.

She didn't need him to say it. She knew he regretted kissing her, and now he was going to pretend it had never happened.

Grace almost collapsed from the surge of emotions that coursed through her body. Every ounce of her being wanted to chase after him like a love-crazy teenage girl, but one look at James, who returned to her side, grounded her. She needed to remember who didn't hurt her or leave her confused, no matter how much she ached for Ty.

"Come on," James held his hand out to her. Her cheeks were flush, and she found it hard to steady herself. If nothing else, she had James.

HOURS LATER, just past two a.m., the party finally began to die down. Grace had sobered up quickly after Ty's hasty departure, and she assumed the busy role of house maid. What else could she do? She didn't want to be the lonely girl sitting in the corner by herself.

Asshole! She thought. She couldn't believe she had returned his kiss.

She efficiently found the trash bags in the kitchen pantry, tucked beneath layers of chip bags and began to collect the discarded beer bottles and plates strewn throughout the house. She stopped for small talk with some of her other employees and accepted numerous compliments on her costume.

The buzz she had been feeling about her appearance had died the moment Ty walked away from her. She wondered if he had gone home. She hadn't seen him since he left the kitchen.

"Hey, Grace, you don't have to do that." James appeared at her side and placed his hand on the small of her back. His touch didn't send the same heat throughout her body as Ty's had.

"It's all right. I feel like helping." She systematically smiled, turning her body so his hand left her back.

He, in turn, placed his heavy hands on her slender shoulders for a massage.

"Really! You don't have to. I want you to enjoy yourself." He smiled, releasing her shoulders to take the trash bag from her.

She caved in defeat, thankful he removed his hands from her shoulders. Now what would she do to keep herself occupied?

"Come here. I want to show you something," James said, interrupting her thoughts. He carelessly pitched the trash bag into the corner of the living room between the couch and the outside wall and took her hand. She stumbled behind him as he guided her back through the kitchen and out the back of the house.

"Where are you taking me?"

"Back here," he answered while he crossed the small deck and opened the side door to the garage. He tugged her inside, making no effort to turn on the light and closed the door behind her. The lack of windows made the garage quite dark, and Grace anxiously waited for James to flip the switch on.

"I want to show you my new toy," he said.

All sorts of horror movie visions flashed through Grace's head as she looked back at the closed door. She resisted the urge to turn the knob and see if it was locked. Then he clicked on the buzzing overhead light, and Grace was flooded with relief.

He crossed the garage and uncovered an antique motorcycle, rusty and mismatched.

"What do you think?" he proudly asked her, tossing the sheet to the side.

"Umm, may I ask what it is?" Her heels clicked on the concrete floor as she walked around the bike, studying it. The bike had no distinct logo or brand name and she couldn't see a badge to indicate what type of bike it was.

"It's called a rat rod. I made the whole thing myself with parts from a whole bunch of different old bikes."

She ran her delicate fingers along the rough edge of the handlebars, which looked very much like the handlebars of a child's bicycle.

"You built this from scratch? Really?"

"Yup," he answered, walking around the bike himself, studying it.

"That's amazing." She smiled and looked at each intricate detail as she worked her way around the bike. The gas tank looked as if it was taken from an early model Harley Davidson and the seat was a newer Corbin seat with custom stitching.

"Why don't you get on?" he suggested with a new light in his eyes.

"Me? Oh, I couldn't. I'd be afraid of breaking something." She smiled and hesitantly stepped away from the bike.

"Have you ever been on a bike?"

"Yeah, I've ridden. I just don't want to mess something up."

"Please, humor me. You'd look amazing on that bike."

"James." It was a warning.

"Look, I saw your kiss with Ty. I'm not stupid. But he also walked away. Please, just give me a shot."

With a surge of courage, she stepped forward and swung her leg over, straddling the bike. It was low, so she didn't have to stretch to place both of her feet on the ground. She placed her hands on the handlebars and looked up at James with a coy smile.

"You look hot," James purred, stepping back to admire her.

She blushed, tilting her head and rolling her eyes.

"No, you're amazing. And Ty is fucking stupid for not taking the chance when he had it."

Grace stood up and climbed off of the bike. "Who said Ty had a chance?"

"Oh, come on. If I hadn't broken the two of you up when I did, you guys would be fucking in the kitchen by now."

Grace abruptly brought her attention to James, realizing the impression she had somehow left on him.

"Watch what you're saying. I don't know what kind of girl you think I am, but I'm not that kind of girl."

Grace didn't know if he was drunk or just being overly rude. She just knew she needed to get out of the garage with him.

"Thanks for the party, but I think it's time I left." She started for the door.

James thrust his expansive body in front of the door, halting her departure.

"Look, I'm sorry. I shouldn't have said that. You're just so hot. And it annoys me that Ty doesn't treat you with the respect you deserve."

"I appreciate that," she answered while trying to step around him.

"He doesn't deserve you."

"I wasn't Ty's to begin with."

"Maybe not, but he's definitely put a claim on you."

"A claim on me?" She rolled her eyes.

"That's right," Ty's voice cut in from behind Grace, causing her to jump. She hadn't heard him open the door. Clearly, James hadn't heard either based on the shocked expression plastered on his face.

"I suggest you leave us now. Grace and I have some unfinished business." Ty stepped further into the garage, his eyes fixed on James with an annoyed expression.

Shit.

Grace's voice caught in her throat as she stood in the middle of the poorly lit garage, desperately looking to James to rescue her.

"Ty, I didn't hear you come in." James took a step away from her like a teenager caught smoking behind the bleachers.

Coward! She turned her blue eyes back to Ty to find embers still burning in his. Her heart pumped harder as her blood thickened with a mixture of anticipation and enmity.

"James, go away," Ty commanded. His intense focus never broke from Grace even as she fumbled to come up with reasons why she needed to leave with James.

James left just as Ty requested. Grace heard the *click* of the door as he closed it.

They were alone. No distractions or anyone to stop the combustion between the two of them.

"Who the hell do you think you are?" She couldn't contain her simmering anger, let alone the hurt his earlier dismissal had caused.

"I won't allow another man to talk shit about me."

"Everything he said was true," she huffed, crossing her arms over her chest.

"Do you really believe that?"

"I do. You don't deserve me. I should have never allowed you to kiss me." Her heart thumped hard against the inside of her chest as her seething anger rose.

"Really? Why is that?"

"You don't respect me."

"You're wrong. I respect you."

Bullshit! Just like Ben respected her?

"Fine. I'm leaving." She turned to leave and ignore the feelings building within her. She was attracted to him, there was no doubt. But her dignity demanded she walk away.

"No. You can't leave. Not until we finish what we started."

"And what have we started?"

"You know damn well what we started. Even James knew what happened," he told her, bringing his hands up onto her arms, so she was closer to his strong body.

"And why would I want to finish? You made it clear you're not interested," she growled. She brought her hands up through his arms to free herself from his touch.

He exhaled and placed his hands on her waist, pulling her snug against the massive force of his unmoving body.

"I didn't make anything clear."

He looked down into her angry eyes, his own eyes searching for something.

"You walked away." She practically whimpered and hated herself for sounding so weak and wounded. Hot tears threatened to stream down her face. Why was he doing this?

"I walked away so I wouldn't do something I'd regret tomorrow."

"So, what are you doing now?"

"Something I won't regret tomorrow."

She lost her breath for a moment. His hands started to burn into her waist, creating the same overflowing pool of fervor she had felt before.

"What if I regret it tomorrow?" she asked.

"You won't."

His mouth was hungry and greedy when he took hers, like a feral cat eating for the first time. Grace felt aghast but turned on at the same time. He expertly caressed her lips, coercing them to give into the lust she felt building. His hands left her waist and buried themselves into her hair, tugging her head back to allow him access to her neck and throat. Her breath quickened as his tongue swirled its way down her neck. She unwillingly let out a soft moan, which allowed him access to a deeper part of her desire.

He had won.

That realization hit her mind like a bucket of ice water, and she immediately shoved him away from her.

"I will regret this tomorrow," she told him and walked back into the house, leaving him standing in the middle of the garage, alone and throbbing with need.

Now, he'd understand how she felt.

DIBS

*T*y woke up the next morning, his head throbbing and his throat parched. He attempted to sit up only to collapse back down after the tightness of his back reminded him he wasn't at home. The lumpy couch he had finally crashed on was unforgiving but after he fell into a deep sleep, he was no longer aware of the discomfort.

He squinted as a single ray of sunshine shone through the partially opened curtains on the window across from him. The house was littered with beer bottles and dirty plastic plates.

"You up?" James' loud voice reached Ty. He turned his head to the direction of the voice and found James leaning against the wall of the living room.

"Yup."

"Hurtin'?"

"Yup."

"Come on. I'll make something to eat."

"Thanks."

Ty didn't rush to get up or follow James into the kitchen. He assumed James wouldn't care how long he'd take to get off the couch.

When Ty sat back up again, he did it slower and took his time down the hallway to the kitchen, making a pit stop at the restroom. Thankfully, he didn't have a sour stomach.

He could smell bacon and eggs. It was a refreshing aroma and a reminder of how lonely bachelorhood could be.

"Thanks man."

"No worries. You're going to help me clean this place up though," James lectured, pointing his spatula at Ty.

"Yeah, I know."

"Grace spent a good amount of time cleaning but it just piled up after she left."

"When did she leave?" Ty asked.

"Shortly after you ran her off."

"Shit."

"You were an ass last night."

"I know."

"No, seriously. You were an ass to me and her."

"Dude, I know," Ty said again.

James tended to the bacon on the stove, the conversation dying for a moment as the meat sizzled and the eggs turned white.

"How do you want your eggs?"

"Over easy."

"So, what are you going to do now?" James asked.

"Nothing. She's made it clear she's not interested in me."

"Are you dense?"

"Why?"

"Dude, she's all about you. But your dumbass keeps screwing up."

"What are you talking about? She hates me," Ty said.

"Well, you don't have a very good track record," James offered.

"Okay. Okay."

"I'm just saying you need to work out this shit with Stephanie and move on."

"Stephanie?"

"Yes, Stephanie. We all know that's why you're being an ass."

"It has nothing to do with Stephanie."

"Bullshit," James said as he placed a plate of bacon and eggs in front of Ty.

"Thanks. And this shit about Steph? That's bullshit. I'm over her."

"Are you?"

"Yeah."

"You sure?" James asked again.

"Sure as you better shut the fuck up before I punch you," Ty threatened.

"Fine. Just trying to be a friend. That's all."

"Well, I don't need your dating advice."

"Why not?" James asked.

"You don't have a good track record either."

"Yeah, I do."

"If you count sleeping with a new woman every night, then yeah, you've got a good record," Ty said.

"Which brings us back to Grace."

"What about her?"

"Is she out of bounds?" James asked.

"Depends."

"Depends on what?" James questioned, as he took a seat next to Ty at the table, his own plate in front of him.

"What are your intentions?"

"What, are you her chaperone now?"

"No," Ty replied.

"Then why do you care?"

"Because I do. She's not a one night kinda girl, anyway."

"Hey, you never know," James said.

"Trust me. I know."

"Eh, you're just not working the charm right. You've been out of practice too long."

"I know just how to charm a woman," Ty argued.

"By threatening her in a garage?"

"You should talk," Ty said.

"She was into me. I could feel it. Until your drunken ass came in."

"James—she's off limits."

"Dude!"

"Dude! She's off limits," Ty repeated.

Ty finished his eggs and stood to bring his plate to the over-crowded sink. The dishes were thrown in like no one who attended James' party cared that someone would have to spend the next day cleaning up.

Ty grabbed the first plate and silently cursed James for not buying paper products. It would have made the whole cleaning process so much faster. Stuck on pizza cheese and what looked like spinach dip was not fun rinsing off with a hangover from hell.

When Ty finished the dishes, which included the pans James used to make breakfast, Ty located a trash bag and began collecting discarded beer bottles throughout the house. He assumed James was responsible enough to recycle and would just empty the bag into the recycling bin. Except he never did find the bin, so he ended up throwing the bag in the large outdoor trashcan instead.

It was well past noon before Ty and James emerged from their cleaning. The house was finally health inspector approved and probably cleaner than when the party started. Ty parted ways and made his way home to indulge himself with a hot shower and a long afternoon nap.

It was the least he could do for himself after the rejection Grace left him with.

MORNING AFTER

*M*onday morning was just as awkward as Grace assumed it would be. Ty was already at the site when she arrived, and she urgently skirted around him. One look at him had her hot blood mixing with her cold mood, creating steam that, at times, felt unbearable.

Her body burned for him, but her mind kept her temperature in check. She needed to remember whom she was dealing with.

James seemed to be on the same page and kept to himself as well. Grace's eyes caught his for a short moment then he shamefully cast his gaze in a different direction.

By ten o'clock, dark clouds had rolled in and it started to drizzle.

"We can keep going. It isn't that bad yet," Ty announced, and everyone continued without opposition.

Whenever Ty came within ten feet of Grace, her cheeks flushed with heat and her gut tightened with anticipation. She hated her body for betraying her.

He was such an asshole.

She tried to put all of her energy and power into her shovel,

119

thrusting it deeply into the earth. She was hot, bothered, and full of more aggression than there was dirt.

"Easy, girl, it's not the ground's fault," James teased from her side, catching her off guard with his sudden willpower to break the ice.

"Yeah, but the ground can take the beating I want to unleash," she admitted, thrusting again.

"Look, about the other night," he started as he cut the ground with his own shovel.

"Save it. Both you and Ty can just go to Hell," she told him with sweat beading on her chest.

James just kept digging.

The rain started to come down harder and the massive droplets formed large stains on Grace's white t-shirt. The rain also matted her hair down onto her face, but she kept digging. At one point she reached her wrist up to swipe her hair to the side with an agitated push.

The water stains continued to create large see-through spots on her shirt, and the weight of the water pulled it tight against her body, although the guys didn't seem to notice. Instead, they had stopped digging and sought shelter as the rain became more violent and pelted their skin.

Grace kept digging.

"Let's wrap it up. Doesn't look like it's going to clear any time soon," Ty's voice boomed from the other side of the site.

Grace continued, ignoring him.

"Grace," Ty called from somewhere close behind her. "Come on. You can quit."

"I'm okay, I want to keep going. I'm on a roll."

He didn't respond, so Grace kept shoveling the dirt.

She heard car doors open and close, the crunch of tires on the ground, and then silence aside from the tapping of the rain through the trees.

Taking in a deep breath, she allowed her body to soften in

the downpour. She tilted her head back for a moment, closing her eyes to enjoy the drops of water that massaged her face. A weekend's worth of anticipation and tension melted away as she stood there in the rain.

"Grace?" Ty's voice broke her Zen-like repose. She swung back down to her shovel and started digging into the ground again.

"Grace." His large hand stopped her arm mid-swing. "Stop, it's pouring. You need to stop."

Her arm sweltered under his intense hold.

"I can still work. It's just rain," she told him and tugged her arm away.

"It's dangerous and a liability."

"I'm not an employee."

"Damn it, would you stop?" He raised his voice and grabbed her arm again. His touch forced a sudden intake of breath.

"Why should I stop?" Grace asked.

"Because I told you to."

"Do you expect me to do everything you tell me to do?" Grace pushed.

"On the job, yes."

"Agh!" She threw her shovel to the ground. "Fine, I'll leave."

"Why are you doing this?" Ty asked.

She couldn't see his face, but she felt his eyes roll. She turned to face him. God, he was succulent. His wet shirt stuck to his carved chest and he was peering at her with beseeching eyes.

Asshole! Asshole! Grace chanted to herself. She had to remember that as her eyes wandered to his chiseled abs.

"Doing what?" she screamed over the roaring rain.

"You shouldn't be here. I agree with your dad now. You're a liability. You don't think. You've already hurt yourself once," he told her and stepped toward her.

"Oh, I see how this works. I rejected you, so now you're going to try and turn my dad against me. Screw you, Ty."

"Grace."

"Don't 'Grace' me. I should be the one running this job. Not you."

Ty stepped forward and attempted to touch her alarmed body when both of their cell phones rang meshing together in that moment.

Grace reached for her phone first with the rain pelting at its screen.

"Hello?"

"*Grace!*" Karen's voice was shaken and she was breathless. "*You've got to come to the office now. Your dad... he's... dead. Grace, he died. Right there at his desk. I'm so sorry. I don't know how else to say it.*"

The phone fell from her hand, plopping into a puddle on the uneven ground. She felt her body sway as the words bounced around inside her head.

Dead. He's dead.

Grace couldn't speak or even react as Karen's voice repeated in her head like a broken record.

Dead. He's dead.

She knew the day was coming, but she didn't anticipate it to be so soon.

"GRACE?" Ty asked as she stood there void of emotion. "Grace!" He reached out to her, and she reacted to his touch with a sudden intake of breath as if she were coming up for air.

She slowly turned her blue eyes toward him, registering his existence.

Dead.

"Grace?" She heard a hint of alarm in his voice.

Tears pooled in her eyes, and she struggled to force the words up her throat.

"Grace?" He lowered his voice to a gentle coo as her frame collided with his, both of them falling to the ground. Grace couldn't hold the weight of her own body anymore.

"He's dead," she whispered, the words escaping her mouth like an exhale.

"Who's dead?" His words rode on a breath as he pulled her against his chest, enveloping her delicate body with his strength. As much as she hated him, she needed him, now, more than ever.

"My dad. He's dead," she repeated as if hearing the words out loud would help them come to reality.

"Tell me where I need to take you."

"The office. Karen told me to go to the office."

"Come on." He half-carried her against his wet chest to his truck, where he opened the door and placed her gently on the front seat.

It was going to be a long, horrible day.

WILL YOU LET ME?

It was dark when Ty pulled onto his gravel driveway later that evening. Grace had fallen asleep against the steel door frame, and her limp body seemed at peace as her chest rose and fell with her steady breaths. Ty watched her for a minute with pity flooding his thoughts. He debated whether he should wake her up.

After leaving the hospital, they spent the afternoon running the necessary errands for her father's funeral. Grace had reluctantly accepted his help, and Ty hoped deep down she appreciated his support. She had refused to eat all day, and he watched her energy steadily decline as the day wore on her. As a final attempt, he had coaxed her to pick up a few groceries with him before returning home. It was a matter of time before she succumbed to the lure of sleep, and he was glad it happened on their ride back from the store.

He knew she'd be mad that he didn't take her back to her motel room, but one look at her restful sleeping body made the decision for him. After the day she had, he wanted to offer her a clean, warm bed and a morning where she wasn't waking up alone. He may have been an asshole, but he wasn't heartless.

The soft *click* of the engine turning off stirred Grace, and she slowly sat up, registering where they were.

"Why are we at your house?" she asked. Ty flinched at her unease. He wished the tension would dissipate.

He wasn't stupid. He knew he was in the dog house. He had been nasty to her. He was angry at the world and women, and he had taken it out on her.

But he also knew that there was something simmering between the two of them that was becoming harder and harder to deny. The mere touch of her had Ty swimming in all sorts of emotions. As much as he hated himself for feeling an attraction, he felt it.

Unfortunately, his drunken state had brought out the worst side of that lust, and now Grace didn't trust him.

"I didn't want you to spend the night alone," he said, hopping out of the truck and gathering some grocery bags from the bed.

She climbed out of the truck slowly.

"I don't want to be here," she said

"I know you don't." He paused with grocery bags weighing down his well-defined arms. He looked into her eyes. "I couldn't leave you all alone in that damn motel."

When she returned his look with an unimpressed expression, he walked past her to the front steps of the porch.

"Ty, please. Just take me home," she said, exhaustion riding on each syllable.

Ty paused at the front door and looked back at her, the grocery bags swaying from his hands.

"How's this? Let's eat dinner. Then we'll see how you feel." He pushed the door open with his shoulder, and heard her footsteps following him.

He unloaded the bags onto the kitchen island and turned back toward her.

She looked lost. The vibrancy in her blue eyes had dulled,

and her face held a hint of white. She looked like she was fighting the urge to collapse. Ty smiled at her. She was trying so hard to be strong.

"It's been a long day. Why don't you take a long, hot shower while I cook dinner? I'll get you a shirt and pants," he offered, settling his hands on her toned arms. He gently smoothed her skin with his calloused hands. Goosebumps rose in their wake.

She pulled away from him with a look of distrust.

"I don't need a shower."

"You were digging a trench this morning. You haven't eaten all day. Please take a shower. It'll feel good."

"I'll take a shower when I get home," she told him and crossed her arms over her chest.

He took a step toward her, tipping his head to the left.

Come out, please, his eyes beckoned to her inner self, begging her.

She held his gaze for a moment then cast her eyes down.

"I'm not trying anything. I just want to help."

Thankfully, she brought her eyes back up to his. They cast a different light this time.

"Fine, but wearing your clothes is where I cross the line." She was amazingly sexy when she crossed her arms over her chest in defiance. Ty had to stifle the smile bubbling up in his chest.

"Seriously, what are you going to put on? Your dirty clothes?" he asked while focusing on unloading the grocery bags.

"I don't care. I don't want to wear your clothes."

There went her arms over her chest again.

He let out a sigh and walked to the neatly organized hallway closet and pulled open the door.

"Here." He tossed some pink fleece pajamas to her. "My ex left those. You're around the same size. They should fit."

She looked down at the obnoxiously pink pajamas. Not

only were they bright, they were adorned with the Victoria's Secret logo across the back.

"Your ex left these?"

"I bought them for her to wear when she came over. She didn't want them, and they were too damn expensive to throw out."

"Thank you?"

"You're welcome. Now, go shower." He didn't mean to sound so bossy, but he was finding it hard to imagine Stephanie and Grace in the same pants.

"And where would that be?"

"You can use mine. It's in my bedroom. Go to the end of the hall; the bedroom's to the right," he explained, pointing.

She left.

He resisted the urge to 'accidentally' wander into the bathroom under the guise that he needed something. He at least knew better than that. He waited for the *click* of the bedroom door, and then went to work to make a nice, simple dinner.

She returned, hair hand-combed and damp, just as he placed their plates on the table.

"You're right. They fit," she announced as she entered the kitchen.

And boy, did they fit—even better than they did on Stephanie. Stephanie was petite, but she had a boyish figure. Grace had curves, very alluring curves.

"So, they do. Come have a seat. I just finished cooking." He motioned to the table and took a seat in his usual chair.

"Thank you," she said quietly as she sat.

They ate in silence. Grace was clearly lost in thought and digesting everything that she had been through.

"What do you think the lawyer will read in the will tomorrow?" she asked, jarring him. The question felt out of place.

The lawyer had called Grace while they were grocery shopping, and she had stepped outside to discuss matters with him.

When Grace returned, she informed Ty that both of them were meeting the lawyer the following morning for the reading of the will.

"I have no clue," he answered.

But he did know, and he didn't want to have that conversation with her right now. Right now, he wanted to enjoy the possibility that she might forgive him.

Tomorrow, they would face the fact that Mr. Evans had left Evans' Construction to Ty.

UNDER THE MOONLIGHT

*G*race was quite shocked when Ty suggested she sleep in his bed. At first, she thought he had balls to imply they sleep together, only to realize that he offered to sleep on the couch. She was so exhausted from the day's events she didn't give the gesture any more thought.

Grace lay down, staring into the unfamiliar room. She felt like a child, afraid of the mysterious but too drained to care. His bed was large, she estimated it to be a king, possibly a California king with a memory foam mattress, or it felt like one. His pillows too were very soft, molding to her head. The furniture looked homemade, designed with a deep mahogany wood, engulfing the room with its impressive stature. Grace noticed the lack of curtains or small trinkets that would have given the room a woman's touch, but attributed it to Ty's bachelorhood.

She tried to close her eyes and allow sleep to overcome her but Karen's words continued to replay in her head, followed by images of her father's lifeless body.

He's dead.

Every time the words formed in her mind, she fought the rush of fresh tears, swallowing the longing that threatened to consume her. She went over her last conversation with her father numerous times, pulling apart every last intrinsic detail to help reconcile the thoughts of regret that consumed her.

She sat up several times, forcing herself to think of something else, anything else that would relieve her mind of the horrible feelings she faced.

After sitting up for the fifth time, glancing at the clock and groaning, she stood up and paced the room. Her feet ran themselves through the plush rug in front of his bed.

He was right. The feeling she was facing would have been worse alone in her motel. She needed some fresh air. With hopes of Ty being a deep sleeper, she slowly opened the bedroom door and tiptoed down the hallway. The front door only had a deadbolt, which she was able to turn without sound. She glanced a peek at Ty asleep on the couch and slipped outside.

The air was warm but held a slight chill in it, forcing Grace to wrap her arms around herself to ward it off. It was a clear night and the moon allowed a perfect nightlight for a glance around his property. The grass was freshly cut, and a clear lawn stretched as far as she could see towards the tree line at the back of his property. Grace inhaled a steady breath, allowing the raw air to fill her tired lungs then exhaled the impeding thoughts that plagued her.

She looked up at the sky, silently asking God for the strength to accept her father's untimely death. In with another soothing breath and out with more unwanted thoughts. Each time she inhaled she blinked to stop tears.

She was looking up at the sky, focused on her breathing when Ty's voice broke her concentration.

"Couldn't sleep?"

She jumped slightly.

"No."

"Wanna talk about it?"

"Not really."

"It's hard. Especially at night, when you have nothing to distract you from the thoughts," Ty said softly.

"I keep thinking about our last conversation."

"Did you fight?"

"Not really. Actually we were talking about you," Grace explained.

"Me?"

"Yeah. I was drilling him for information about your mini-vacation."

"I wouldn't call it a vacation."

"He was so impassive. I remember yelling at him, 'You need to care that Ty just took off without notice.' Then he told me, 'Why? He's trying to close some loose ends so he can focus on more important things. Like you.'"

"He was right."

"You can't just take off."

"But I *was* closing loose ends so I could focus on you," Ty said.

"Me?"

"Yes, you."

"Stop."

"Fine, this isn't the right time. But we'll have to talk about this."

Grace shook her head. It was an involuntary response to him.

"I'm going back inside," she declared.

"Okay. Do you need anything?"

"Sleep. I need sleep."

"Well, good night. Again."

"Good night."

She pushed past him and walked back down the hallway, her feet feeling heavy with fatigue. Maybe now she could fall asleep.

LETTER

"Mr. Evans requested that I give both of you these letters before we begin. I will give you twenty minutes to read them and then I'll return to continue with the reading of the will," the attorney advised both Grace and Ty as they entered the posh conference room of the highly priced attorney the next morning. With a polite smile, he handed each of them a crisp sealed envelope then left the room, closing the heavy glass door silently behind him.

This was it. This was the beginning of the end.

When Ty had brought Grace home last night, he dreaded the point that they had now gotten to. She preferred being alone during one of the most difficult parts of her life instead of being with him.

Now, his apologetic eyes searched for hers. Her expression went pale when the attorney handed her the letter. She was fighting back tears. This was it. This letter and subsequently the reading of the will afterwards were going to seal Grace's hatred toward him.

In that moment, the past couple of months flooded his mind, and he realized what he had done wrong. He should have embraced her, lifted her up, and accepted her. The chemistry they felt was something different. But he was too hurt and too stupid to acknowledge it.

"I'll go out in the hallway to give you some space," Ty explained, standing to depart. Their eyes still hadn't met, which caused the tear in his heart to expand.

"Thank you," she responded, her eyes never leaving the white envelope in her hands.

Ty left the glass walled room and settled in the brightly lit hallway, holding his own letter which he knew would seal his future.

Taking a deep breath, he slid his finger underneath the closure, breaking the bond it had on the underside. Once it was open, he pulled out the single piece of folded stationary paper.

The letter was in Mr. Evans' handwriting.

Dear Ty,

If you are reading this, then the final stages of my cancer have taken my life. You have been like a son to me, and I couldn't have asked for a better employee. Because of our close relationship, I have decided to give both you and Grace equal partnership of Evans' Construction.

Now, I know Grace won't like this decision.

You will manage the construction aspect of the business, and Grace will manage the business aspect. As a team, you two will thrive.

In order for both of you to maintain your ownership in Evans' Construction, you must marry Grace within a year of today's date, or the business will be sold to an interested third party.

Yes, I said that correctly. Marriage. I want my daughter to be a happy woman married to a man I know will treat her well. I know you can be that man.

I love my daughter, and I want to see her happy. I know you can make her happy, and you deserve to be happy too.

Thank you for everything you've done for me these past ten years. I hope someday you will come to understand why I did what I did.

Until we meet again,

Bill Evans

TY LEANED against the textured wall, steadying himself. He was overwhelmed with the weight of the information he had just read.

Marriage. Bill Evans wanted his daughter to find love with him. Since when did he decide that Ty was the man for that job, and what was he going to do now?

He took in a stabilizing breath, composed himself, and walked back into the naturally lit conference room.

Grace sat at the table, her delicate face reflecting the same shock Ty felt. She didn't look up when he walked in, but continued to study her own multi-page letter.

He pulled a leather chair out; the sound of the rollers gliding across the marble floor broke the stillness of the room. His eyes looked up, searching for hers again.

This time he was presented with a pair of very scared and panicked blue eyes.

A slight curve appeared on his lips, which was reflected on hers. As he settled into his chair, he didn't know if he should speak or just remain silent until the attorney returned.

"Marriage?" she asked.

"I'm sorry," was all Ty could drum up in reply.

"Sorry for what?"

"All of this."

"So, did you two have enough time to read your letters?" The attorney's voice boomed as he appeared in the room.

"We did," both of them answered.

"Good, so let's get started." He pulled out a plush leather

chair at the head of the table, unbuttoned his suit jacket, and sat down.

Two hours later, Ty and Grace mutely left the room side by side. Ty held the door open for her and walked with her down the main steps of the office to the rear parking lot.

"So, either way, I never gain full control of my father's company," she commented as she fished something from her purse.

"Grace." He stared at her, begging for her attention.

"Why would he make me marry you? You hate me." She finally looked up, becoming aware that he was staring back.

"Why would you think I hate you?"

"Oh come on," she retorted. She turned towards his truck.

Ty followed behind her. He needed her to look at him. He wanted her to see the pity and sorrow he felt for her. He needed her to understand this wasn't his fault and he was just as blindsided as she was.

"Why would you think I hate you? I don't hate you."

He noticed her sharp intake of breath. "You're so confusing. You kiss me, then discard me. I don't know what to think."

"I want you, trust me, but that's the problem."

"Why is that a problem?" Her voice cracked, and her bottom lip began to quiver.

"I can't do a relationship. Not now. Not after Stephanie."

"You know what? Just take me home, please." Tears cascaded down her flushed cheeks before she turned to hide them.

He took in a deep breath and turned her around, pressing her to the side of his truck with his body. He cradled her face and tilted her head so that his lips could claim hers. Her body was rigid at first, but he persisted until she began responding.

And when she responded, his body went wild. Her lips parted like a spring flower opening with morning dew. Her tongue teased his by coming out and retracting like a fish in hiding. She tilted her head slightly to allow him better access to her lips which were becoming plump with need.

His lips parted from hers to plant feather-like kisses along her jawline and down her neck, creating goosebumps in their wake.

A very soft, almost muted moan slipped past her lips and teased his ears.

"I want you. I want to try and make this work," he growled, sucking harder on her neck.

Another unexpected sigh rushed past her lips, and she arched her back, allowing her breasts to press against his chest.

"Ahem." The sound of someone behind them took a moment to break the trance between the two of them. Ty tore his lips from Grace's throat to meet the eyes of Mr. Evans' attorney.

Damn.

"You two have a great evening." The attorney nodded towards them with a knowing smirk on his face. Grace's cheeks grew flushed and she took a shameful step away from Ty.

Shit.

DINNER PLANS?

*W*hat the hell just happened? Grace took in a deep breath as the attorney's office faded in Ty's side-view mirror.

Grace felt so confused and overloaded with emotions. She worried she was going to explode like a shaken can of soda.

Ty sat silent in the driver's seat, his focus on the road. The lines on his face appeared filled with regret and it felt like he was purposely focusing on his driving, instead of turning to her periodically like he would in the past. The weight of his contrition started to fall onto Grace's shoulders and she found it too uncomfortable to sit next to him.

"Can you just take me to the office?" she asked, biting into the rich air with her soft voice.

He glanced over at her, his expression unreadable, then pulled the truck over to the side of the road. She took another deep breath.

"I'm sorry I keep fucking up," he told her and placed his warm hand on her exposed knee. Electricity presented itself at the site of contact and, as if Ty held a direct line to her core, the contact created a puddle of heat.

"Can we please just go to the office?"

"If that's what you want," he said and returned the truck to the asphalt. They didn't share another word.

~

THE USUALLY ACTIVE office was quiet when Grace walked in the front door. She didn't wait for Ty to follow.

"Hello, Karen," Grace said as she made her way toward the back office.

"Hi, Grace. I tried calling you," Karen stated, spinning in her desk chair to talk to her.

"Did you? I didn't hear my phone ring. I'm sorry." Grace pulled her phone out in surprise.

"It's not a problem. I didn't know if you were coming in or not."

"Well, I'm here now," Grace said.

"So, how'd the meeting go?"

"It went, it just… went."

"Did you know?" Karen asked.

"Did I know what?"

"That we have to get married," Ty's voice cut through the office like a jet airline.

"Did I know? No. I had no clue."

Ty stood at the front pass-through window overlooking Karen's desk as if he was waiting for her permission to come in.

Grace didn't offer it, just turned and headed down the simple hallway to her father's office. She had to remain focused. If she allowed her mind to wander in the slightest, it would think about that kiss, the amazing, emotion infused kiss that had her blood boiling and her gut tensing.

Remember what happened after the kiss. He regretted it.

Grace shook her head, trying to expel the thoughts

bubbling up, and moved around the cluttered desk, determined to focus on the daunting task ahead of her.

She heard his cat like steps as he followed her into the office.

"Ty, I really need to be alone, please."

He instead approached the other side of the large, dark mahogany desk.

"Go make rounds at the jobs. I really need some time alone."

He just continued to look down at her, his apology hanging high in the room. He leaned over, the muscles rippling in his forearms as he braced his powerful body on the edge of the dark wood.

"What do you want?" she asked.

"How long are we going to play this game?" His hand brushed the underside of her chin, bringing her gaze up to his eyes.

"I can't do this right now."

"Why not? Now's just as good as any other time."

"I… we need to get a grasp on the company before things spiral out of control." She looked down at the set of plans on her father's desk.

Correction: *her* desk.

Ty bent down further, bringing his face within distance of her breaths.

"You're right, but first, we need to settle this."

"I can't. Not now. Riverwalk? What's left to do at the site?"

He responded with a slow, seductive kiss.

Fueled by grief, confusion, and lust, Grace responded. She returned his kiss with a rhythmic flow of her lips against his. He swiftly deepened the kiss against her willing lips, invading her body with an overwhelming heat.

His tongue danced with hers, encouraging her to blossom against him. It rolled and teased, generating an intense emotion deep in her gut. No, not emotion: it was an intense need, a craving. A craving that brought on fear.

Grace tore herself away from him. She couldn't do this. Not here. Not now.

"You need to stop! I can't do this. Not now."

He backed off without any further resistance.

AFTER FOUR HOURS of plumbing into the depths of her father's business, Grace and Ty came up for air. Those depths seemed to hold a lot of hidden jewels Grace hadn't been aware of, such as a lot of profit from past jobs and a vast array of clients who were still waiting for work to commence. They couldn't have asked for better circumstances to take over a business.

Grace reached for her cotton jacket on the back of the chair and walked around the desk to face Ty.

"I'd like to take you out to dinner," he told her, taking her jacket to place it on her shoulders.

"Dinner?"

"Yeah, dinner. Is that okay?"

"Nothing more?"

"Not unless you'd like more."

Grace exhaled. She wasn't up for the mental sparring he seemed to present.

"I don't understand you. A week ago you rejected me, and now I can't keep you away from me," she said and stepped away from his fingers, which seemed to linger on her shoulders longer then they needed to.

"Look. Both of us have been through a lot. Can we just start over?"

"Start over? Or do you want to start over because you know what's at stake now?"

"Are you kidding me?" He threw up his arms up in exasperation.

"Well?"

"Grace!" He thrust his hands through his hair. "Please. Don't make me beg. Both of us aren't ready for marriage, but we have to try or both of us will lose everything."

Bingo! There it was. She was right.

He stood there shaking his head as he studied her. His hair had become mussed from his frustrated tousling, and she could see the adrenaline coursing through his veins as he struggled to keep his posture calm.

Marriage. That damn word.

As much as she hated the idea of conceding to him, he was right. If they didn't try and make things work, both of them would lose the business.

He tipped his head to the side as she debated with herself, stewing over the idea of being married to someone who clearly didn't want to be married. His expression changed, frustration and desire mixing together as she resolved it within herself.

"I'll ask again: dinner?" He reached his hand back out to her.

WE'RE ADULTS

*T*y struggled to keep his damn libido in check. As she sat across from him at her father's desk, all Ty could think about was the annoying craving for her lips. As she spoke, he was focused on them, noticing how moist and plump they were. His eyes widened when her tongue periodically crept out to remoisten them, leaving a light dew across their surface.

He knew she was struggling to keep herself focused by constantly bringing his attention back to the stupid plans on the desk. He didn't want to talk about work or what was happening at that damn job site. Instead, he wanted to spend the afternoon exploring her amazing lips.

If looks could kill, that attorney would be lying dead back at his parking lot. Ty couldn't believe the man broke the moment he was sharing with Grace. And it had been broken. Grace had run from him with her tail between her legs. She'd even questioned his feelings.

He had to admit that he was surprised when she suggested his change of heart was because of the will. Of course, the will played a major role in his decisions now, but marriage? Was he really ready for marriage? Attraction was there. There was no doubt in his mind. But marriage? Could he really commit himself to Grace?

He witnessed the wave of contemplation cross through her eyes before she replied, "Fine, I'll go with you to dinner. But no more kissing." She stood and led the way out of the quiet office.

"Grace." He reached out and stopped her, lightly touching her arm. "I'm not just doing this because of the will."

She shuttered her eyes, making it very difficult for Ty to read her emotions.

"Ty, you had your chance, and you blew it," she calmly told him as her eyes met his with raw hurt.

"I don't think I blew it. I just need to show you the kind of man I really am." He slid his hand down her arm and tugged her closer to him. The heat of her body radiated onto his, and his blood started to simmer. She didn't turn away from him and the air caught in her throat as her eyes stole a glance at his lips, tugging at his groin. He took in a sharp breath and lowered his lips onto hers.

Her body went rigid as their mouths connected, and he brought his hand up to cradle her face, directing her deeper into the kiss. She relaxed slightly, responding with a reservation he understood and respected.

"Let yourself go, Grace," he urged her, speaking the words against her mouth.

"I can't. You'll only hurt me. You don't want this, Ty."

She delicately pushed against his chest, breaking the connection.

"I won't hurt you," Ty said, trying to reunite their lips.

"Let's get something to eat. You're not thinking or acting rationally," she told him and pushed against his chest again. This time he stumbled backwards, more out of shock rather than her strength. The cream colored wall in the hallway stopped him from tumbling to the ground. She was rejecting him.

Fuck!

"All right, I understand." He took her hand with caution, and guided her out of the office. Dinner it was.

The restaurant Ty chose was a small, quiet place on the outskirts of the city, named Longdoggers. It was an outdoor restaurant with metal tables and a Tiki bar. The air was warm and fans created a soft breeze in the outdoor seating area. Grace sat calmly across from him, studying the laminated menu while he studied her.

"I think I'll get the pineapple chicken. It sounds good." Her voice erased his sporadic thoughts like a blow dryer erasing steam from a mirror.

He smiled at her.

"What are you going to get?"

"The same thing I always get, steak and a beer," he answered, concentrating on her face. She blinked and lowered her gaze to the shellacked table, then she toyed with the edge of her napkin.

"Do you come here often?" she asked.

"I do, at least once a week."

She lowered her gaze to the napkin again.

"I don't know anything about you," she admitted.

"What do you want to know?"

"I don't know. What do you like to do?" she asked, continuing the assault on her napkin.

"That's a loaded question," he teased, meeting her hand at the napkin.

"No, it's not. You're making it a loaded question."

"I like to work on my house. I like to hunt. I like to fish. I like all the things guys like," he answered with a smile reaching his eyes.

The waitress returned with their drinks.

"What about you?" Ty asked.

She thought for a moment as he studied the strand of hair that escaped her pony tail.

"I like to read. I like camping. I like..." She paused.

"Camping? I like to go camping too. Let's go next weekend." She opened then closed her mouth.

"What? Do you have plans?" he asked.

"No, I just don't think camping is a good first date."

"Oh, so you're inviting the idea of a first date? Why not camping? What a great way to get to know each other."

"Ty!"

"What?"

She smiled, and a blush stained her face. "I'm not going to share a bed with you on our first date."

"Oh, come on. It's not like we're sixteen and I'm asking to take your virginity."

Her face turned pale and a shot of embarrassment shone in her eyes.

"Wait," he said, tilting his eyes to make contact with hers again. "Are you a virgin?"

"What? Are you kidding me?" she immediately responded, redness spilling onto her cheeks.

"Well, are you?"

"Ty, seriously. What do you think?" Her innocence was shining through the small golden specs in her eyes.

They had kissed several times. That was it. They never had had the opportunity to explore anything further than a kiss because, much to his annoyance, they were interrupted each time. She was a determined woman; there was no doubt in his mind. But as he studied her, looking deeper into her eyes, he noticed something he hadn't seen before, innocence.

So, was she suddenly insecure because she was ashamed of being a virgin, or was she insecure because she wasn't and was ashamed to admit her promiscuous behavior?

Oh, the plot was thickening.

"I think the fact that you won't answer my question leads me to believe I may be right."

He knew she was a couple of years younger than he, but to really believe she was a virgin in her late twenties, he was having a hard time swallowing that lump. There was no way. But as he continued to look at her, her bright red cheeks and crossed arms implied that he was right.

"I'm not a virgin," she answered, shaking her head very nervously and avoiding eye contact.

"Why do I think you're lying?" he teased and reached across the table to take her hands in his.

"I'm not lying."

"It's okay if you are. It doesn't bother me. I won't go running for the hills." He smiled again, tilted his head, and tried to meet her diverted eyes.

She rolled them, then brought them defiantly to his.

"You idiot. I'm not a virgin. I just don't freely have sex with every guy I'm attracted to."

Oh, the sudden temper was sexy.

"Wait. Does that mean you're attracted to me?"

"I didn't say that."

He had forgotten that he was holding her hands until she started to pull them away. Subconsciously, he tightened his grip, clasping onto her delicate fingers. Her eyes challenged his, and she tried to free her hands but failed.

"Ouch," she announced, like a toddler's response to a tickle attack.

He playfully tightened his grip.

"Ty, come on," she told him, continuing to wiggle her way out of his fingers.

"Oh, I'm sorry." He clutched them again and brought them to his mouth to brush his lips across each knuckle.

Her tongue peeked out again to moisten her parched lips.

He could hear her sudden intake of breath when his lips reached her last knuckle.

"Ah, there's that attraction again."

"Ty?" The sound of his startled and loudly spoken name caught him off guard, and he lifted his eyes away from Grace to determine where it had come from.

He knew that voice, and the moment he laid eyes on its owner, he paused.

"Stephanie," he cursed under his breath as the familiar face approached the table. He dropped Grace's hands onto the table. She looked amazing, wearing a simple red summer dress with her short hair brushing her shoulders.

"What are you doing here?" Ty asked her, all of his senses honing in on the one woman who made the ache in his heart stop.

Well, one of the women. Grace faded behind him for a moment, only a moment, as he bathed in Stephanie's courteous attention.

She looked amazing, as she always did. Ty turned his body to her.

"You look great," he said, reaching out to take her hand. Then reality threw a running animal in front of his speeding car when her fiancé appeared at her side.

"Ty," he said as he extended his hand out. Ty studied the man's feminine hand for a moment before accepting it in a powerful handshake.

"Bryan," Ty responded with the same bored tone.

Grace bluntly cleared her throat, and when Ty didn't react to the sound, she stood. Her chair scraped loudly across the concrete floor.

"Grace?" Ty asked, feeling lost and confused as all the stars began to disassemble and create chaos in his body.

"Please excuse me. I need to use the ladies' room." She smiled politely. Her chair continued to scrape loudly across the floor as she made her hasty departure.

"Grace? That is the Grace you were talking about?" Stephanie asked, pointing to her departing figure. Ty watched as she walked away. The feeling in his gut threatened to eat him whole.

"Yes, that's her," Ty regretfully responded.

As he tried to maintain a pleasant and light conversation with the woman he had centered his whole life around, he subconsciously monitored his internal clock, waiting for Grace to return. Ten minutes and a very boring conversation passed while Ty's ears honed in on anything that would indicate that Grace was returning. He periodically stole glances in the direction she had left, hoping to see her brunette head reappear. Another moment passed, and Stephanie was going on and on about the date of the wedding and where they thought about having it.

Ty couldn't care less.

That was supposed to be his wedding.

Stupid bitch.

Five more minutes passed. Now he could feel the temperature rise in his body as the anxiety built and pounded inside him like a wave pool at a water park.

"It's been great seeing you. I'm happy for you both. But you need to excuse me. I need to check on Grace." Ty cut right through Stephanie's tirade about seating arrangements and moved to depart.

"Oh. Okay. Well, I hope everything is all right."

"Me, too."

Ty scanned the restaurant for Grace. He wondered if she had been stopped by someone she knew or maybe she had forgotten where they were seated.

No luck.

When he reached the ladies' room, he looked around then knocked on the door.

"Grace?" he called through the wooden door.

Nothing.

He pushed the door open a little bit.

"Grace!"

Nothing.

He looked around to make sure no one was watching, then slipped past the door.

"Grace?"

The room was empty. He rushed outside, looking for her little, red, fireball of a car. It was no longer parked next to his truck.

Shit.

REBOUND

race unlocked the door to her crappy motel room. The outside light finally burnt out because it seemed darker outside than usual. She needed to hunker down and find another place to live. Her father had left her more than enough money to find a more suitable place to call home. He'd left his primary residence to her step-mother, which was fine. Grace got the business.

Well, she got the business for at least a year.

She unloaded her purse onto the small round table by the front window and headed back to the bathroom. She needed a steaming hot shower for her frozen nerves. What the hell was she going to do now? Her father was forcing her to marry a man who clearly had feelings for someone else. Hadn't her father known that?

She stepped out of her clothes, leaving them in a heap on the bathroom floor, and turned on the faucet. The sound of running water filled the small room.

Thoughts of Stephanie plagued her. She was a beautiful woman. Her red hair had framed her face perfectly and lightly brushed against her bare shoulders. Grace almost felt jealous, and her heart still stung from Ty's sudden dismissal. Grace had been thrown to the side as the spotlight shifted from her to Stephanie.

Grace climbed into the questionably clean shower. The rush of heat soothed her chilled skin. She tipped her head back into the falling water and washed away the feelings of rejection. As far as she was concerned, anything that had attempted to blossom between her and Ty had died. The weed killer known as Stephanie saturated it at the roots. She couldn't, no, wouldn't marry someone who could so easily cast her aside.

Grace's shampoo filled the foggy bathroom with a milk and honey scent as she worked it up to a lather against her aching scalp.

Her eyes released burning tears as she rinsed the scented soap out of her hair.

Why was she letting him hurt her so much?

She let out a harsh sigh and poured a generous amount of conditioner in her palm, running it the length of her sleek hair. The sound of her phone's ringtone drifted from the other room. She knew it was Ty.

Finally, she rinsed the orange and lily body wash from her skin and turned off the shower. Her phone persistently rang as she continued with her nightly grooming routine, taking her time to floss her teeth and apply lotion to her thirsty skin.

When she left the bathroom with a towel wrapped around her head and her thick fleece bathrobe encasing her body, she dug into her purse for her phone, accidentally spilling it and all of its contents onto the floor.

"Shit," she cursed under her breath as she followed it to the floor. A knock sounded at the door as she scooped up her items.

Grace wasn't surprised or startled. She expected Ty to show up and apologize for his behavior. She took her time finishing her task at hand and stood to approach the door. A more impatient knock sounded again.

"I'm coming! Hold on," she called out to him.

She slowly unlocked the door and cracked it open; she planned on only allowing a few words to pass.

He looked like hell. No, worse than hell. Ty looked like a defeated man who had taken the beating of a lifetime. His basic black polo shirt was wrinkled, and his khaki pants had some creases in them from sitting in a chair all day at the office. He combed his hand through his tussled hair, avoiding eye contact.

"What?" She was harsh, but her heart wanted retribution for his actions.

He kept his gaze down, not speaking at first.

"Ty, just go home," she said attempting to close the door.

He reached out and pushed the door back, his large muscles flexing and stretching his sleeve as he brought his tortured eyes up to hers. He kept his arm on the door, just above her head.

The closeness of him made her breath catch in her throat.

"I'm sorry," he spoke, his voice deep and low. He cleared his throat with his eyes digging deeper into her.

"Of course, you are. You have a lot to lose." She tried to push against the door with her body.

He released his arm from the door, and he rounded his body so that his free hand could cup her face, defeat heavy in his eyes.

"Ty, please."

This was too painful. It was worse than her breakup with Ben and they had been more than intimate.

"I'm so sorry," he pleaded, stepping into her. He brought his face mere inches from her freshly washed cheek.

She could feel the warmth of his breath against her skin. Slow tingles crept up her neck as her body became aware of his. She shook her head and took a step back, her foot catching on the welcome mat just inside the door. She fell backwards, struggling to regain her balance, and landed on her back with her bathrobe parting at the waist and gaping open at her chest.

Ty's eyes went wide like a teenager seeing porno for the first time, then he stepped farther into the hotel room, bending down to offer his help in getting up.

Grace's chest rose and fell as she struggled to cover her body, embarrassed at her misstep.

She accepted his hand. He politely shifted his eyes toward the back of the room as she adjusted her bathrobe.

"Please understand how sorry I am for what happened."

"What's done is done."

"I'm sorry. Really. I don't know what came over me."

"I do. You're still in love with her."

"I'm not in love with—"

"Bullshit! You threw me to the side like roadkill the moment she stepped up." It was blunt and really harsh, but it was the truth and Grace was tired of skirting around the truth. Why her father had sentenced her to such damnation was beyond her, but she knew one thing for sure, he still loved Stephanie and today reinforced that.

"Why did you leave me there?" His pain was obvious and as much as Grace wanted to help ease his pain, she couldn't admit out loud that she had left because his rejection stung like a nest of hornets or that she felt sub-par, ugly, unwanted and rejected.

"Did you leave because you think I still want Stephanie?"

She still couldn't admit it out loud.

"Grace, I realized today that Stephanie isn't who I want."

"That's bullshit."

"I'm serious. I realized I don't love her anymore."

"That's hard to believe."

He closed his eyes and released a very painful looking breath.

"Grace, I'm falling in love with you."

Grace stopped breathing. Her body went limp and cold as

she backed herself against the bed, seeking it for stabilization. She didn't feel angered by him anymore. The tension that was building dissipated the moment that word left his lips. No one said anything about love. That was crazy.

Her mouth went dry, and it felt like a cat's tongue had replaced hers.

"You can't love me," she spoke with shallow breaths. He lusted after her just like most guys did. No one ever mentioned the L word.

"Why not?"

She pulled the edges of her robe tighter against her chest and attempted to feel comfort in the blanket it was providing around her body. She resisted looking at him, apprehensive of how he would react to the connection.

"Why not?" he asked her again from across the room, his eyes pleading with her. He looked so lost and raw.

She sank back further into the side of the bed.

Because he loved Stephanie.

"You don't love me. You may be attracted to me and may even have feelings for me, but you don't love me," she explained, attempting to ignore the throbbing building in her core.

"Grace, I've been in love. I know what it feels like."

This was crazy. He couldn't love her.

"You love Stephanie."

"Not anymore. I realized that today. When you left, all I could think about was you. I worried about you. Not her. You."

"No. I'm not going to be a rebound."

"Grace—"

"I think you should go." She pointed toward the door.

He stood up effortlessly, straightening his shirt and his pride. Then he came to her and brought his hand under her chin, lifting her eyes to his.

"I'm not going to give up."

She got lost in his eyes for a moment, wishing it were simpler.

"I am," she told him and placed her hands on his flat abs to keep a distance between the two of them. The simple connection jolted a spiraling wave of sensation between her legs. She didn't mean for it to happen, but it did. The whole room seemed to dim as she realized the spark her fingers started.

"Let me show you that I mean it," he pleaded and reached up to cradle her face again. She blocked him and backed away.

"You don't need to show me anything. Just leave, please." She pointed at the door.

"I'm not giving up," he told her again as he opened the door and looked back at her with intense eyes.

"I know," she whispered under her breath.

With that, he left, leaving the room cold and lonely. That loneliness was something Grace knew she needed to face in order to protect herself.

The next morning, Grace anticipated Ty showing up at work with flowers and a charming attitude. She figured he would woo her and do everything in his power to prove his point. Except he didn't show up, evidently going straight to the job site. He didn't show on Tuesday, or even Wednesday either. His parking spot remained empty each morning. So, Grace did what she knew best and plunged into the never-ending pile of paperwork on her desk.

Without even being asked, Karen deflected many phone calls by telling the callers that Grace was in meetings or away from the office. Thankfully, that kept Grace busy enough to keep thoughts of Ty at bay.

Then on Thursday, Alejandro, one of the carpenters, arrived at the office.

Apparently, he had been told to get some papers from Grace with the layout and color choices for the partitions in the men's restroom. Alejandro's presence solidified Grace's suspicion that Ty was avoiding her.

"He needs the email from Niles that explains the layout of the partitions. I guess there are questions about the layout and colors," Alejandro clarified for Grace. She was trying to remain focused and unaffected by Ty's blatant disposal of her.

"I guess he's meeting Niles in an hour to discuss them," Alejandro continued as Grace scrolled through her computer for the e-mail with the layout. He sat patiently in the chair opposite Grace's desk.

Grace continued to scroll through the communications, looking for anything that would pertain to the partitions, and printed them out.

"Thanks." He smiled, taking the folder of printouts when she finished.

"You're welcome." She paused for a breath. "Do you know why Ty didn't come here himself?"

"I don't know. I don't question when Ty asks me to do something. I learned to just do it," Alejandro said with a grin and bounced up from his seat.

"Oh, okay." Grace smiled back.

"I do know this. He told me he screwed up, and he's going to make it right. Whatever the hell that means," Alejandro politely added.

"I figured that much."

She returned to her desk as a signal that Alejandro was free to leave.

LATER THAT NIGHT, she lay in her uncomfortable motel bed, searching her iPad for places to live. There had to be some place better than where she was. A place that didn't offer critters for roommates or burnt out lightbulbs. The television was flashing scenes on muted volume, and she clicked on the bedside table lamp to get a little more light in the room as her right hand scrolled.

Zillow didn't offer much in the way of homes. All of the three-bedroom, two-bathroom homes were either too old, too close to each other, or too boring. She was prepared to shut down for the night when she came across a listing she didn't expect. She clicked on the link and studied the pictures of the house.

It couldn't be—not after all the blood, sweat, and tears he'd invested into it. But it was there, clear as day with a huge *For Sale* sign on the front lawn.

She remembered the smoothness of the granite counter tops and the detail of the cabinetry in the kitchen. She flipped through eighteen pictures of his house, concentrating with awe. She couldn't believe it. Ty's house was on the market.

LOVE OR LUST

*L*eaning against his hot truck, Ty took a sip of his melted ice water. He took a moment to breathe and relax after another accomplishment filled day. The trees were serene as a soft breeze wafted through them, and the water sparkled with the afternoon sun. To his surprise, a pair of dolphins splashed in the water close to the new dock, and he stood straighter to gain a better view. The water parted around their fins and followed them as they bounded in and out of the water.

He was sad that this job was coming to an end, but he was very pleased with the outcome. It was a beautiful park, and he was proud to be a part of such an improvement for his community. He hoped there would be many dolphin sightings in the future.

As he turned to collect his things, a familiar red-hot car pulled onto the gravel behind him. His heart began to crunch with the gravel below her tires. He wasn't ready to face her just yet. Her rejection still stung too much. But he knew her better than that. He figured it would just be a matter of time before she came. He wasn't avoiding her, though he knew that's what she assumed.

He was just giving her the space that she demanded. He had screwed up. He knew it the moment Grace excused herself to the restroom. He was faced with a pivotal moment in his life, old versus new, and he was the dumb-ass who chose the old.

He should have known better. He should have focused on Grace. But at that moment, he didn't know where things were going between them. He didn't realize Grace had feelings for him until that moment.

And he blew it.

"Hi," she spoke. Her voice was flat and short. She unfolded her shapely legs from the car and placed them gently on the gravel. Her skirt slowly rode up her legs as she bent to stand.

He swallowed the lump in his throat and forced his eyes to remain amicably on her face. She watched him and immediately broke the connection between their eyes to pull her skirt back down her legs.

"Hi," he returned, fighting his gaze from traveling south.

"Why are you selling your house?"

"How'd you know?"

"Doesn't matter. I want to know why you're selling it."

"Because it was a house for Stephanie."

Grace stepped back for a moment. She placed her hands on her hips and studied him. The silence created major anxiety deep in Ty's heart. He was drastically changing his life for another woman, and he hoped this time he had made the right call.

"You can't sell your house because of her. You've put too much heart and soul into it."

Then he witnessed the wave of realization as it washed over her, and guilt began to stain her cheeks. "Do you think if you sell your house that I'll change my mind?" she asked, her voice hesitant and cracking with guilt.

"Isn't that what you want? You said yourself you didn't want to be a rebound. So, I'm unloading my baggage," he told her with more truth than he intended.

She sucked in a breath, the air gliding across her teeth. She was clearly taken aback by his words.

"What I want shouldn't matter."

"Why not? I told you how I feel." He took a step toward her.

"But it's not real. What you feel for me isn't real."

"Says who?"

"You're in love with Stephanie. You can't love me."

"I realized the day you left me that I never loved her. I loved the idea of her. But she didn't love me. She wanted me to become someone else. Even when I did that, she still didn't love me." Grace opened her mouth to speak but he continued, "I'm not done. I know you're worried and you think you're a rebound, but I assure you that's not what's happening."

She crossed her arms over her heaving chest and let out a loud sigh. She was determined; he had to give her that.

"I told you I would prove to you that my feelings were true, and selling my house is the first step in doing that."

He reached out and placed his hands on her arms, stabilizing her. Her body went rigid at his touch, and her innocent eyes remained fixed to the ground.

"You can't love me. You don't even know me."

"But I do know you. I know that you're stubborn and determined. I know that you feel this annoying need to prove yourself and be the best at everything. I know that you're drop-dead gorgeous, even when you're sobbing in my arms." Ty was cut off by her soft, strawberry Chap Stick lips.

"Shut up," she said against his lips.

They'd kissed on several occasions, but this one was different. This one was raw with the pressure of need forcing its way through each of them. Grace's arms wrapped around his neck like she needed his undivided attention to confirm her fears weren't justified. Ty invited her enthusiastic greed and allowed her to consume him.

Her lips were soft and supple as she deepened their kiss with every movement. He enjoyed the exploration of her hands as she climbed the terrain of his body as each fingertip felt every plain and valley.

Ty ran his hands through her loose hair, tangling them deeper into its mass. She moaned as he tugged her head back, and he placed his desperate lips upon her neck.

"I want you," he growled.

Then she shoved him away, throwing off his balance. Alarm raced through his veins as he tried to comprehend what was happening.

"See, it's just lust," she stated.

Ty regained his balance and moved toward her departing body, confused by her last statement.

"How can you deny that you feel it too?"

He'd had enough of this game. She showed all the signs of a wanton woman. Her lips were plump as blood filled them, enticing him. Her eyes had become more dilated, focused on his body. Her voice had become deeper, more seductive.

Yet, she didn't react and that made his blood run thicker. He couldn't be that mistaken. He'd been with many women and he knew what lust looked like. She may be lying to herself but her body wasn't lying to him.

His hand met her arm, and he spun her around, blood pulsing deep in his ears.

"No. You're wrong," he said and secured her petite body against him. It was a gamble. He didn't want to scare her or push her too far.

She looked up at him, her pupils still dilated. It was there. His body had been responding to it since the moment they met.

Lust.

She was accusing him of lusting after her, yet when he looked deep in the pools of her eyes, he saw it there, smoldering. As much as she deflected him and as hard as she tried to hide it, his body had honed in on it, and now his libido was summoning her to let go.

"You can't tell me that you don't feel it too."

"Lust? Yes, I feel it. But common sense taught me that if I give into it, I'll get hurt."

And there it was. Her reason for denying herself the endless pleasure they could enjoy.

She was afraid.

And she had every right to be. He'd pushed her away so many times, why would she think this time was different?

"Come with me," he directed, tugging her toward the newly constructed dock. It was the perfect setting. The sun was providing him with an amazing backdrop, and they were finally alone. No distractions. No one to interrupt them.

It was time he showed her how he felt rather than telling her.

It was time he let go.

There was tension in her arm as he aimed her towards the end of the wooden dock.

"Please."

His simple request seemed to release her and she allowed him to reel her in, positioning her in front of him. The water below the deck was calm and afforded them serenity. Each step brought them closer to the end, closer to their destination and the final goal both of them needed to achieve.

"What I'm feeling for you is deeper than you realize," he hummed into her ear as he brought her to the gangway.

The sun was setting fast, and its final rays danced against the water, making the glass top sparkle with different shades of orange and pink.

A canvas painter's tarp lay against the floor at the end of the pier. Earlier that day, Ty had made some last-minute touches to the handrail, and as if Ty knew that he was returning, it lay there like a welcome mat.

His arms blanketed her body as they approached the tarp, pulling her firmly against his growing front. A single word didn't pass between the two of them, yet a whole conversation seemed to unfold amid their joined bodies.

Her wispy hair smelled like a faded shower, and her body molded perfectly against his.

He brought his lips close to her right ear, "Let me show you," he whispered.

She turned her face toward his lips, allowing him to place a simple yet intense kiss on her temple. Like a cat wanting attention, she rubbed her face against his lips and closed her eyes.

"Ty." His name came out like a light breeze. "I'm afraid you'll break my heart," she admitted, breathless, yet determined. She rolled against him, turning her body so they faced one another.

Ty smiled down at her, his nose teasing hers. "I wouldn't dream of it." He brought his left hand to the small of her back, while his right tilted her chin up so she could see his sincerity.

She slightly tilted her chin, closing the distance between them. The crush of her lips indicated her surrender. She was offering her trust.

Her lips were expectantly soft and pliable, and he proceeded with caution, treating her like a delicate flower.

"Trust me," he moaned as he deepened the kiss between them. His hands seduced her skin, moving in an ancient dance, summoning her to enliven with him. And she began to rouse, slowly unfolding the layers of fear.

She steadily transformed into a vixen, enchanting him with slow seductive movements of her curvy body, gyrating her hips against him, rocking them against his growing need.

Deepening their kiss even further, Ty bit on her lower lip

and suckled on the tip of her exploring tongue. A soft, bewitching moan escaped her mouth, and she returned the gesture, nipping at his lower lip.

"Mmm, maybe I was wrong about your innocence," he teased against her swollen lips as he swayed with her body.

Grace bravely brought her fingers up and tugged on his collar. The motion brought him closer to her.

"I told you I wasn't…" she paused for a moment, building the intensity of her next words, "…a virgin."

She thrust herself against him and entwined her arms around his neck. With his hand still on her lower back, Ty effortlessly lowered the two of them onto the stiff painter's tarp. Her chocolaty brown hair poured around her face as she lay expectantly below him.

"Oh, I believe it now," he smiled and arched upward to remove his shirt. He threw it on the bench across from them, his eyes never leaving hers, unaware that he overthrew it into the water instead.

His tanned chest was puffed with adrenaline and need. She looked delighted as she gazed at him as her hands cat-pawed at the rigorous muscles of his torso.

"You are amazingly hot," she cooed, traveling her hands to his belt. Her blue eyes locked with his through her forest of eyelashes.

Ty was astonished by how seductive this woman could be. His body had sensed this side of Grace long before he realized he was attracted to her. She was courageous, fully surrendering her trust to him.

He returned the sentiment with another kiss. This time he pulled her wide-collared shirt to the side so he could trace kisses along her collarbone. She struggled to maintain her caresses against his torso but lost the battle as he pulled the collar of her shirt wider to expose her hot pink bra.

"Can we lose this?" he asked her, caressing her swelling breast with his hand.

Grace attempted to sit up, eager to remove her shirt, only to have Ty restrain her.

"Only your bra, leave your shirt on," he suggested with a mischievous grin.

She returned his grin with a seductive look of her own. Her plump lips curved in a knowing smile.

"Then you'll have to acquire it yourself," she teased, a bedeviling smirk growing on her face as she returned to her reclining position.

"You sure you want me to do that?" he asked, focusing his attention on stretching her shirt back against her shoulder.

"Don't let me regret it," she said, brushing her hand against his growing need.

Ty smirked at her efforts and thrust his hands up from the bottom of her shirt below her bra and made contact with the bare skin of her engorged breasts. His thumb and finger clamped her nipples, twisting the sensitive tips and forcing her to buck as a sudden jolt was sent between her legs.

The collision of her hips against Ty's manhood forced a moan of pleasure from his lips.

Ty maintained his position on her breasts, removing her bra and continuing the sensuous torture until he couldn't take her bucking any longer.

He released the swollen tips and returned his focus to kissing her.

"You are so beautiful," he said, encasing her body between his arms.

She smiled, her eyes fixed on his as she lifted her shirt from her body and threw it to the side.

Ty surveyed her flawless bare skin, enjoying the perfect curves of her willing body. Then, knowing the exact amount of time he was allowed to ogle, he lowered his naked chest to hers, reveling in the feel of her nudity against him. He kissed her lips, her neck, and her collarbone again, then casually brought his mouth to each nipple, suckling them back into heightened peaks.

Grace covertly worked on releasing his belt, skillfully gliding it through the loops of his pants until it was free to be discarded. Then her fingers magically released the button of his pants, and he suddenly felt her dainty fingers wrap themselves around his throbbing manhood.

"I don't have much experience, so you'll have to seize control," she cooed with persuasion, seduction heavy on her words.

She wanted him. She was practically begging to be taken. This was it. This was the moment he had been waiting for.

He paused for a moment to take in the magnitude of the moment and revel in its significance. This was it. He was finally moving on.

Grace must have sensed his hiatus and promptly paused below him as her hand stilled on his engorged cock.

"Ty?" Her voice was light and simple, yet held back a whole world of fear.

The dismay in her voice snapped him back to the present.

He could see the need clouding her eyes as her lips swelled with anticipation.

"I'll seize control and give you pleasure that you never even knew you could feel," he boasted. His smile grew bigger with confident pride. Her wall of fear crumbled before him as she began to relax. The emotion was all over her angelic face. All she had ever wanted, from him, from her father, was acceptance, and acceptance is what she would get from him.

Her dainty hand remained on his throbbing member, and as if both of them realized it at the same time, she brought her lips down to him with a coy smile.

"No," he directed, pulling himself from her plump lips and swinging her up to meet his mouth.

Smiling with his eyes, he yanked her jeans down and off her legs then brought his head down to taste her flowing nectar. She tried to stop him, shyly shaking her head and smiling with an innocent denial as his head sunk below the valleys of her legs.

"Ty, I don't like that," she admitted, trying to summon him back to her face.

Where had the vixen gone? Where was her confidence? Had no man ever given her pleasure, or was it always one-sided?

"Don't like it or never had a man do it?" Ty challenged, remaining between her smooth legs.

Her cheeks turned a sexy merlot with the innocence an instant answer. The revelation was an amazing turn on for Ty. He had never been with a woman who didn't like to be pleasured by his mouth. In fact, they all came to beg for it. She didn't want to answer his question. He could tell. It was extremely hot.

Grace, the take-charge pit bull of a woman, was embarrassed. He reveled in her modesty for a moment. Then he plunged in, parting her blue lace panties and gorging himself with her sweet nectar.

She timidly screwed her eyes shut.

Ty couldn't believe how such a simple act made her so demure. Then, very slowly, she began to wiggle as he worked magic with his tongue. Though she seemed embarrassed, her body reacted to the pleasure, releasing more nectar for him to enjoy.

His eyes monitored hers, summoning her to open up and experience the pleasure with him. As he pleasured himself with her sweet juices, soft moans escaped her lips, and she brought her hands up to her face to hide them.

Her hips nonchalantly rolled and swayed as the familiar

tide started to build within Grace. Her hands abandoned her face, and she latched onto the painter's tarp to stop herself from soaring.

"There you go. Release it," Ty encouraged her, expertly licking at her nectar and swirling his tongue in ways he knew would bring her to the explosive peaks he had promised.

Her body started to tense, and she screamed out as the sensational drive pulsed through her body.

"Ty!" she screamed out, and his name rolled on the wind.

He brought his face back to hers, gratified with his work. He urgently initiated kisses as need built in his body. His bare chest crushed her engorged breasts as their naked bodies molded together.

"Please, Ty. Please take me," she begged. Her lust filled voice was foreign to him.

She still wanted him, wanted to connect with him.

Thank God.

Ty obeyed without hesitation, thrusting himself deep inside her, expanding her and increasing her release.

She cried out in a surprised, pleasure-drunk moan, clawing at Ty's back as if she was trying to bring his body closer, deeper into hers.

Ty felt his own release climbing, and his logic shone through for a hesitant moment.

"I don't have protection," he explained in an alarmed rush as his climax threatened to boil over.

She continued to thrust her hips, sinking him deeper into her body.

"It's all right. I can't get pregnant," she explained in a breath-less slur.

That's all Ty needed to hear before his lower regions took over. He swelled larger, expanding her further, and released with an intense flow inside her.

His excited moan was accompanied by her satisfied whimper, and he crashed on top of her, all energy expelled from his fulfilled body.

"Grace, I love you," he whispered into her ear, kissing her cheek gently.

"I love you too."

She loved him too. Ty's smile radiated from deep within his soul.

"I don't know where my shirt went," he smiled down at her, deciding it was time they left before a police officer found them.

"I think you threw it in the water," she teased, rubbing her exploratory hands against his bare chest.

"Shit. I think I did." He smiled at her. Then he picked up her shirt and tossed it into the river.

"Ty!" She stood up to chase after him, her naked body tempting him.

"Well, if I have to go home shirtless, so do you," he mocked, teasing her breast with his hand.

Grace frantically gathered her remaining clothes before he decided to discard those as well. "If you go home shirtless, it's safe. Plus, you're a guy," she playfully reminded him. "If I go home shirtless, I'll attract the wrong kind of attention."

"Then don't go home. Spend the night with me," he suggested, stepping back into his jeans.

Grace paused and studied him for a moment. He wondered what thoughts raced through her head. Was his offer too soon? He strutted over to her, shirtless and hot, placing his hands on her hips, beckoning her to look back into his eyes.

"As a matter of a fact, why don't you live with me? It'll be safer and a hell of a lot more comfortable," he suggested, the words sounding so at ease coming off his lips.

Grace took a step back, using her panties as an excuse to create the gap between them. She slowly placed each leg into them, deep thoughts creasing her forehead.

Then she pulled on her jeans, creating a show as she swayed each inch up her incredible legs. She didn't speak, didn't respond. Finally, she smiled as she picked up her bra and latched it back into place.

"I have a better idea," she said, returning her body to his. "Why don't I buy your house?" She smiled with pure determination flushing her face.

JOB APPLICANT

*B*uy his house? What the hell was she thinking? Why did she say that? Of course he wouldn't sell his house to her. That would be crazy. Maybe it was the sex. Maybe it was her desire to get the hell out of that scum-hole of a motel.

She didn't know. But the words escaped, and she couldn't take them back. Neither could she take back the complete look of shock plastered on his face. Damn it. She'd ruined the moment.

Ty painfully searched for the right comeback. She could almost see the gears in his mind grinding against each other. She had to allow him to rebut. It was only fair.

"Why would I let you buy the house I built for someone else?"

Dumbass, Grace cursed herself.

"I don't know why I said that." She felt her cheeks simmering with heat.

He cocked his head slightly to the side and smiled at her. Thank God, for that jaw-dropping smile.

"How's this? You move in with me so you can get out of that

hell-hole motel, and we'll look for a place to buy together," he told her.

"Shouldn't there be a marriage before we buy a house together?" she said without her words fully thought through, again.

"That's what I hope. And I guess that's what your dad hoped too," Ty clarified.

Oh, how Grace hated her father right now. Always spoiling the moment and reminding her there was no way what was happening between the two of them was natural.

"We'll see," Grace answered.

A WEEK after their intimate moment, Grace found herself looking for a distraction to conceal the anxiety that was erupting inside her. Ty had been the perfect gentleman all during that week. He took her out to lunch each day, filling their meals with meaningful conversation and plastering on so much chivalry, Grace was going to implode with annoyance.

Yes, she was a woman and holding the door open for her was a sign of respect, but he didn't have to pull her chair out for her, place her napkin on her lap, and pour her drink. It was degrading.

So, on Friday afternoon, after they returned from another smothering lunch, Grace felt herself cringe when Ty followed her to her office. She needed to address what was happening between the two of them.

"Hey, I've got to go out to the church. They came across more rot, and the guys want my direction. Will you be okay?" The question was so heavy with respect that the weight finally made Grace's facade crack.

"I'll be fine. I'm more than capable of running this business without you."

The surprise that shot into his eyes immediately made her regret her outburst. She didn't mean to sound so harsh.

"Okay," he said, backing away with his surrendered arms in the air.

Before she could fix anything, he was gone.

Shit.

She debated whether she should call after him, but Karen settled the dispute with a beep of the intercom.

"Grace, I have someone here who would like to apply for the project manager position," Karen announced.

"Karen, we're not hiring at the moment," Grace replied with a firm press of the intercom button.

"Ty asked me to place an ad last week," Karen replied.

Grace sucked in a long shallow breath and audibly let it back out. Fine. She'd meet with the man out front and deal with Ty's lack of communication later.

"I'll be out in a minute," Grace informed Karen and released the red button on her phone.

She stepped into the private bathroom in her office and studied the mirror for a moment.

Her hair was in place, and her teal shirt was crisp and sharp looking, even though she felt like someone who hadn't slept in days. Each step to the front of the office was deliberate and thought provoking. Maybe Ty was right. They needed help. They were drowning.

But who was he to make that call without even asking her first?

As she turned the corner to greet the man applying for the project manager position, she took in another settling breath.

He stood as she approached, and his expectant face fell the moment their eyes met.

"Ben?" His name came out as a gasp, and Grace stopped short from entering the lobby and settled her feet on the cold tile floor.

"Grace." His voice was laced with shock, but Grace assumed it was fake. He attempted to gain authority with his tone. He was good with using authority. Grace had firsthand experience with that. Still, she stood motionless for a moment, unable to form words. Her mind started a whirlwind of memories and flashbacks.

"Grace?" His voice cut through the slideshow and cleared a path for Grace to direct her thoughts.

Ben Lindy.

"Ben, we're not hiring." She threw her words at him.

"Is that so? When I spoke with Mr. Parks, he implied that I had already been hired." Ben crossed his arms over his thin chest. Compared to Ty, Ben was thinner with a leaner body. Ty had more bulk and mass in his defined muscles, making him manlier to Grace.

Grace stood taller and brought her blue eyes to meet his cold gray globes. It had been a long time since she had seen that chiseled face. She'd wondered how she'd react to him or the aura of attraction that seemed to always cloud around him.

"Really?" Taking a step in his direction, she said, "Well, Mr. Parks is not the owner of this company." She looked him square in the eyes, determined to not back down.

"Seriously?" He didn't hide his disappointment with her defiance.

"Yes, and it will be a cold day in Hell when I hire you," she answered, placing her hands on her hips.

"Then it must be a cold day in Hell. Isn't that so, Mr. Parks?" Ben answered, a smug smile forming on his lips as his focus shifted from her eyes, to her chest, and eventually behind her. Grace spun around to find Ty opening the front door of the office. Ty looked like a history teacher unable to answer a question about history, with his eyes wide and caught off guard. He smiled politely to Ben and extended his hand for a shake.

"Hey, Ben. I'm sorry. I haven't had a chance to talk to Ms. Evans about your employment," Ty explained and placed his hands on each of her shoulders to indicate who she was, completely unaware of the situation that had been unfolding.

"Gotcha. That would explain why she didn't know you had hired me," Ben said, slathering on heavy disrespect towards Grace as he spoke. He kept his hawk-like eyes on her.

"Well, I'll make it simple for all of us. Ben, I'm sorry to inform you, but you don't qualify for this position. Thank you for your efforts, and we wish you the best of luck," she answered, placing her hands on his biceps to redirect him toward the front door.

"Wait! I'm sorry, Ben. I need to talk to Grace, can you come back tomorrow?" Ty asked as he stepped between Grace and Ben in an attempt to diffuse the strange situation. He really was clueless and probably thought she was mad that he'd tried to hire someone without talking to her first.

"Sure. You can handle her and call me whenever." Ben shot Grace an annoyed glance before exiting the building.

"Get your hands off me!" Grace angrily growled at Ty before rushing down the hall toward her office.

"Grace! What the hell?" He followed closely behind her.

"What the hell is right? Who gave you the authority to hire someone?" She turned to face him, pounding her finger on his hard chest.

"I figured we needed help. And you seemed so busy, I thought I could find someone for you. I knew Ben from one of our subcontractors," he answered while struggling to keep his voice even and nonthreatening. He knew he'd stepped in shit, he just didn't know how bad it stunk.

"Well, that's all great and dandy, but there is no way in hell I am working with Ben Lindy," she answered as she turned to take a seat and ensure he couldn't read too much on her face.

"What's wrong with Ben?" He continued to follow, taking a seat in the chair across the desk from her.

"The answer is no."

"Why? Ben would be perfect. He knows both of us, he's got experience, and he graduated from UNF," Ty's voice no longer hid his annoyance.

"Ty." She brought her innocent eyes up to meet his from across the desk. "I was in the hospital for several days because of him."

SAFE

*T*y was so blindsided by that heavy fact that he almost fell back in his chair.

"What?"

"Ty, don't make me repeat myself."

He stood up, walked behind her desk, and took her slender arms into his hands. He needed to touch her, to feel the warmth of her body, and to know he wasn't hallucinating.

She refused to look up at him, as if she were ashamed. But how could she be ashamed when a man hurt her; and even more, how could she stand so strong in the same room with the very man who did it?

Hell, the rage building inside Ty right now was so strong he had to hold onto Grace and ground himself before he chased Ben down in the parking lot and beat the living shit out of him.

"You've got to repeat what you just said so I know for sure I heard it correctly," Ty told her in a calm and authoritative voice. "This isn't a simple matter."

Grace brought her capable eyes slowly up to meet his. They held an affirmative power as if she had come to a resolution of the matter a long time ago.

"Yes. Ben Lindy beat me so bad one night that I ended up in the hospital. We were together for six years... six years and in a fit of rage one night he beat me unconscious because he thought I was cheating on him. He is the reason my father didn't want me in construction. He is the reason why my father is trying to force me to marry you because my father was afraid I'd go back to him."

Ty stood there dumbfounded and void of all intelligible responses. He didn't know how to react. He didn't know what was appropriate. It was too much information flooding him at once. Everything seemed to make sense now. Bill Evans was trying to protect his daughter. He was afraid Grace would cross paths with Ben again.

He opened his mouth to speak when Grace brought her fingers to his mouth and silenced him. The steady hold her eyes held on his kept him silent.

"I don't need you to be a knight in shining armor. I don't need sympathy. I am not a victim. I left and I've moved on," she said.

But Ty wasn't hearing her. His mind was caught in violent rapids of emotions, thoughts, and memories. He thought about the night on the dock and the intimacy they shared. Was he too forceful? Did he hurt her then?

He reviewed every movement in his head: her soft legs, her wild hair, and her warm belly. There was no warning. She gave herself to him fully. She hadn't acted like a victim.

Or had she?

He was always raw with her: kissing her with a reckless abandon at James' party, stalking her at her motel afterwards, and kissing her at the lawyer's office. He was always forceful, determined. He couldn't contain the primal need of his craving for her. He never realized the impact his actions had on her.

Now he felt ashamed for placing her in those positions. She was a victim, and he fell into the role of abuser.

"I am so sorry. I didn't know. I had no clue," he said and took her into an apologetic embrace to express his regret physically. She pushed herself away from him.

"Don't do that! I'm not a victim, so don't treat me like one."

"But he hurt you!" He couldn't begin to imagine hurting a woman like that.

"Ty!" She let out a frustrated sigh and placed her palms at her temples to ease the frustration building in her head.

"No! I won't tolerate this. You can't just accept that someone beat you. How often did it happen?" he continued. He felt he had to do something, change something.

"Ty!"

"I mean, that's abuse! That's just downright fucked-up. And that asshole thinks he can demand a job from you?" Ty started pacing her office as anger coursed through his body.

"Ty!" He wasn't even hearing her fragile voice as rage flooded his ears. He needed to rectify things. He needed to make things right for Grace, for Mr. Evans, for himself.

"I'm going to ruin him. I'm going to make it so he can't have sex ever again, that fucker!"

"*Ty!*" This time her voice cut through the room like a fire alarm and pierced through Ty's angry haze. Ty turned and refocused on the beautiful woman in front of him.

"Just stop. Please. If you want to make things better for me, just stop," she pleaded. Grace was pleading with him.

Did she ever plead for Ben to stop? Did she cry herself to sleep? Did he care that he hurt her?

"Ty, stop! Stop thinking about it. Please." Her face had turned pale and her blue eyes were threatening tears.

"I'm sorry. I can't help it. I can't imagine hurting you like that," he told her, cradling her lovely face in his warm hands.

"Then don't because you wouldn't. You aren't that kind of man. So don't try and understand it. I chose to be with him. I consented to that relationship. I also chose to leave him. I focused on my career. I haven't been with anyone since him until you. And you were gentle and kind, and you made me feel safe," she told him as she pressed her cold hands against the stubble on his cheeks.

He smiled, relief washing over him at her words. He made her feel safe. He'd done it right this time.

"Grace, I love you," he admitted to both himself and her. It was the truth. He loved her more deeply than he had ever loved Stephanie. He felt a raw connection with her. She made him feel complete.

"Ty."

"Marry me not because of your dad or the business but because I love you," he continued.

"Marry you?" She seemed stunned.

"Yeah. Marry me. Be my wife. So you can be safe for the rest of your life."

"No."

Her answer wasn't spoken with venom or any hint of rudeness, but it packed a huge punch.

"No?"

This scene was feeling way too familiar.

"Yes," she answered, her firm tone seizing any chance to change her reply.

"Yes, you'll marry me?" he tried again.

"No, Ty. I won't marry you," she answered, turning from him.

God, those words hurt. They stung like hot oil splattered on his face. He wanted to ask why. He wanted to grill her until he understood the reason for her immediate response. But she didn't allow him to. Instead, she turned toward the back of her desk and grabbed her purse.

"Where are you going?" Ty asked her, annoyed that she was acting so aloof after dismissing his heartfelt proposal. Didn't she see his heart flopping on the floor?

"I don't want to have this conversation here," she answered and brushed past him.

"Okay, so where would you like to have this conversation?"

"Just come with me," she answered without turning back to see if he were following.

Karen didn't say a word as both of them walked past her desk.

"Ty and I will be out for the rest of the afternoon. We have some legal stuff to deal with. Can you please take messages and tell them I will return on Monday?" she asked as she walked by the front pass through window.

"Sure. Anything else?"

"Nope. You can close up, right?"

"Yeah. Don't worry. I've got it."

"I know you do. Thanks. See you Monday." Grace opened the door and walked to the parking lot. Grace didn't speak as she unlocked her car and climbed in. Ty didn't know whether to follow her or get in his own truck.

"Come on. Get in," she called to him.

Ty felt so out of balance. He didn't know what to do or how to approach the situation. It was crazy.

Grace didn't speak as she drove apparently in her own world. He could see the concentration on her pale face. She was trying to come up with the right words and was actively working on it.

Her body was stiff and tense. She was stressed and showed fear as they drove.

"Where are we going?"

"Away. I needed to get away. I need to clear my head and wrap my thoughts around everything that's happening," she admitted with her eyes trained on the road. Her fingers were gripping the steering wheel and twisting along the black leather braiding.

"Grace, I—"

"I was a virgin when I met Ben my senior year of college. I was young and very naïve." She continued to twist her hands on the wheel.

"You don't have to explain anything." Ty placed his hand on her arm. She tensed up and continued her focus on the road.

"He swept me off my feet, showered me with attention, and promised me he would take care of me. And he did. After a couple of months, I expressed interest in having sex. That's when we had 'the talk'. He explained to me that he was a sadist and that sex with him would be the most amazing and thrilling sex I would ever experience, but I would have to follow his rules. I seriously thought I was on the set of *Fifty Shades*. It was thrilling, and each time we were together was more and more intense."

"I don't want to hear about your sex life with him." He couldn't listen to anymore. He didn't want to know how much she enjoyed being with that monster.

"You need to understand."

"I don't need to understand anything. That man ruined you. He hurt you. He doesn't deserve to even breathe the same air as you."

Grace pulled the car over to the side of the back-country road. The sun shone through the bright green leaves, creating a peaceful ambiance for the afternoon.

She took in a deep breath, breathing in courage as well. "I consented to that relationship. I enjoyed being his submissive. That's what I need you to understand. Yes, he hurt me, but after six years of that type of relationship I started to enjoy the pain. I ended the relationship because the hospital called my father and he forced me to end it."

"Do you still love him?" Ty needed to know. Had he misread her all along? Did she ever have feelings for him?

"Not anymore. He was mad that I ended our relationship for my family's sake. He expected me to disown my own family, even after I ended up in the hospital. He didn't think he'd done anything wrong. Sure, he apologized but I knew I had to get out then or I'd be trapped forever." Raw pain seeped from her words. "When you're a submissive, you put one-hundred percent of your faith in your partner and trust that they will always take care of you. He didn't do that. When he hit me because he was angry, he crossed a line that he shouldn't have crossed."

Ty didn't think Grace could shock him any more than she already had, yet he was swimming in a pool of knowledge that threatened to drown him.

"Ty, I love you. I can honestly admit that. But I can't expect you to commit yourself to the real person I am. I have been trained to love and be loved a certain way. Something most people cannot understand. I don't believe you or I can find real pleasure because of my past."

"What about our time on the dock? Didn't I please you?"

"Yes, but that was the first time I've had sex with anyone like that. The first time I wasn't tied up or experiencing pain. I enjoyed it, but I was also scared out of my mind," she admitted.

Ty sat back deeper into his seat. He didn't know what else to do. He was flabbergasted. The information she had shared threw him so far off course that he didn't think he'd ever be able to see the lighthouse again.

Most men liked to be in charge. Ty took pride in taking care of the women he was with. He embraced the leading role. But Grace was talking about a whole different level. It was a different type of leadership, one where he took her whole life into his hands.

He couldn't hurt her. He didn't see pleasure in that.

What was he going to do now?

SUBMITTING

The following week was a blur for Grace. She tried to avoid Ty at all costs, and he seemed to feel the same need. Her heart ached for him. She ached for his unsolicited attention, and she missed the light banter that always followed. But she had closed that door.

That's what she wanted, wasn't it? Her father had tried to force marriage upon her. How could she love someone she was forced to marry? Yet somehow, she felt the ping of attraction and craved his presence.

Somehow, he had found a crack in her wall and had slipped through it.

Somehow, she had fallen in love.

They hadn't spoken in a whole week. Ty had kept to himself when they were in the office, and Grace had buried herself in projects and hoped her dedication would pay off. They had two months before her father's deadline loomed over them.

They had two more months until they were to marry or lose the business they had poured their hearts into to some stranger who didn't know anything about the business.

A light knock on her office door broke Grace's concentration. She looked up, expecting to see Karen and was startled when Ben stepped in.

As always, he was perfectly groomed, which suggested a perfect life, a perfect life she knew wasn't so perfect.

It had been almost two years since she had been involved with him, since she had wholeheartedly handed her soul and trust to him. Having a relationship like that was deep and intense.

Now, she looked at him with a haze of mistrust. This very man was the cause of her demise. He had broken her down to her basic elements and destroyed the hope that she carried for a happily ever after. She had been pure and innocent until she willingly gave herself to him. She had been an angel handing herself to the devil.

He stepped cautiously into the room in an action foreign to him. Ben never treaded lightly. This immediately put Grace on alert.

"Ben?" His name was more a breath rather than a word.

Grace mentally surveyed the office. Karen had gone home for the day, and Ty had been missing in action for days. She was alone.

"Grace," he spoke with more authority than his actions showed. He seemed to be struggling to assert himself. Again, it was something that was foreign to him.

Grace stood up. "What do you want?" she asked, forcing a threat in her words.

He let out an exasperated sigh almost like a growl and narrowed his dark eyes on her. This was the Ben she was more familiar with.

"It seems as though it's not what I want but rather what your boyfriend, Ty wants," Ben stated as he advanced toward her with determination.

Grace unconsciously took a step backwards and bumped into the wall behind her desk.

This didn't go unnoticed by Ben, and a smirk formed on his lips.

"What is that supposed to mean?" she asked, removing herself from the wall.

"He expects me to give up my bid for your company in two months. He wants me to sign over the rights solely to you," Ben started again. This time he stepped around the desk so he was in her personal space.

Her lungs deflated, and she found it difficult to refill them. Her father hated him. There was no way her father would have willingly given his company to Ben.

"You're the 'interested party'?"

"Yes, I am."

"But how? My father hated you."

"Your father didn't know that General Construction was owned by my uncle, who planned on giving your company to me. I also didn't know that your father owned Evans' Construction until I came in to apply for a job last week."

Grace gripped the sides of the desk and strained to regain her composure.

"Why did you come to apply for a job if you plan on buying the business?"

"I wanted to see how things worked and to determine which employees to keep. What better way than to go undercover as the new guy?"

Ben took a step closer, his large frame towering over her. It was an action he used all too often when he was prowling after her. He would ignite the sexual flame that burned in her belly when he stood so close with his eyes cast down upon her.

Grace straightened herself and stood defiantly.

"So, you didn't know that the company was to be willed to me?" she stated rather than asked him. Her eyes then accidentally focused on his lips, a habitual action.

It was habit. She was falling back into a habit. She told herself that.

"I knew the company was to be willed to the owner's daughter, but only if she married. I didn't know that daughter was you. Once I realized it was you, I knew the company would be mine. I knew you wouldn't be marrying anyone. I tried to give you the opportunity to submit to me. However, it looks like freedom has lit a spark of defiance in you."

Submit to you!

Those single words froze over Grace like an ice storm taking over a forest. Her whole body went rigid, and the snow that had begun to strangle her mind suddenly vanished.

"Submit to you! I don't even trust you anymore. I will never trust anyone ever again because of you, you fucking asshole." She unleashed her temper and stepped toward him with a force that made him step back.

"Excuse me?"

"You heard me. I trusted you. I handed my whole soul over to you because I trusted you so much, and then you hurt me. I don't think I can ever love again because you broke my trust so completely!" The rage spewed out of her mouth with such intensity that she needed to step back and take a deep breath.

"That's why you still need me because no other man can love you the way you need to be loved. You won't have to work if you're with me," he told her.

"Are you kidding me? I'll never return to your fucked-up life. You can go find some other innocent girl and break her." Grace shoved him. Her rage drove her to continue to hit him until she drew blood.

"Grace! Stop!" His voice didn't register at first. Grace could only hear blood flowing violently in her ears as she swung one arm then the other. She hit Ben anywhere they landed.

"I won't stop! I want you to feel the pain you caused me!" she screamed and continued her assault.

"Grace!" This time his voice held a deep authority, a threatening one. It was a voice she knew signaled that she had gone too far. That voice used to mean pain. Except she wasn't consenting to that type of relationship anymore. She could walk away this time.

So she slowly backed away, deflecting her gaze from his, and attempted to steady her breathing.

"Do you feel better now?" he asked her in a deep husky voice.

She couldn't believe it. He was turned on by the fact that she was unleashing her anger on him.

"No! You can leave now."

"Are you sure you want me to go?"

"As sure as the day I walked out on you," she answered.

GETTING DIRTY

*J*t was Friday evening, and Ty needed to unwind before he exploded from stress and built-up lust. He had gone all week without speaking to Grace, giving her time to think. He wanted to respect her, and right now he knew the only way she would expect him to behave was to give her space.

And he hated it. Every time she walked by he had to fight himself from reaching out to touch her, caress her, or even to brush his fingertips on her delicate skin. It was too much. He was denied another marriage, and he didn't think his heart could handle another rejection.

The sun was slowly lowering itself behind the tree line as he maneuvered his four-wheeler through the muddy trails behind his house. Mud: it was raw, dirty, and all male.

And at the moment it was splattered across every exposed and swollen muscle on his upper torso, and it felt amazing. He loved to go out and ride when he was mad. Somehow the unclean act of drowning himself in mud pit after mud pit helped evaporate the stress that he had carried with him all week.

The goggles that framed his face were intact; he thrust the throttle back one more time and flung mud up and around himself through the last mud pit directly behind his house. His jeans were almost completely covered with the thick brown substance as he ended his final fling for the night. He stopped in his back yard with mud dripping from his body, the vehicle coated completely, and lifted his goggles from his face and placed them on his head.

"Do you feel better?" Her voice cut through the distance as if she had spoken right in his ear.

Ty looked up and focused on the house; stopping in awe at the beauty standing on his back porch. She had changed into simple jean shorts and a white t-shirt like that night at the bar. They were such simple clothes, yet when combined with Grace's long tan legs and slender body, they had major sex appeal.

"Not really," he admitted with a smile.

She walked toward him with purpose; her hips swayed as she approached.

"Well I don't feel better either," she told him as she stopped inches away.

"Would you like to go for a ride?" He didn't expect her to take him up on the offer.

So, he practically jumped off the seat when she hiked her right leg over the back of the four-wheeler and pressed herself against his naked, muddy back. Her white t-shirt was no longer white. Instead of questioning her actions with the shock that coursed through his veins, he only reached into the side pocket and handed her a pair of clean goggles. She smiled and accepted them. He watched her as she carefully placed them over her clean face. Then she pulled her hair into a messy ponytail and smiled at him.

He didn't speak. He didn't need to. She had come to him, and he would wait until she was ready to talk. Right now, he was going to focus on getting dirty with her. He twisted the throttle and flung them across the back lawn and back into the trails. The sun had almost disappeared behind the trees, but the moon was large and acted like a bright flashlight.

Grace's arms snaked around his exposed waist, and the feel of her delicate fingers splayed across his hard abs sparked interest in his libido. As he kept his eyes trained ahead, his mind conjured images of her mud-stained white t-shirt. A simple smile formed on his lips. Life couldn't get any better than this: out riding, getting dirty, and sharing it with a beautiful woman he had fallen in love with.

Wind flew past them as he sped through the trails and whipped the back end to try and get her muddy. She giggled from time to time as a large puddle of mud would splatter across her skin. Her exposed legs were slowly becoming slathered in the thick dirt, and the smile that remained on her face made Ty's heart flutter with love. "Can we stop for a minute?" she yelled over the motor of the four-wheeler. Ty stopped almost immediately along the narrow trail.

"You okay?" he asked immediately. He worried he had gone too fast or gotten her too dirty.

She stepped off the back of the four-wheeler and stepped away. She didn't bring her attention to him or attempt to speak. Ty climbed down and slowly approached her.

Shit. Did he ruin the moment?

Mud clung onto his naked chest like it was afraid of falling as he reached out to touch her. She was cast in the moonlight with mud staining her perfect face.

"Yes," she stated, out of breath and not providing anything further.

"Yes?" Ty was confused. Yes, she was okay?

She stood up straight and turned her blue eyes to him.

"Yes, I'll marry you," she answered.

Ty startled for a moment. Had he heard her correctly?

"Yes?" He needed to hear her repeat it again. All week he had prepared himself for rejection. He assumed he had gone too far, and there was no going back.

Apparently, he was wrong.

"Yes," she answered with a bright smile.

Excitement flashed in his veins, and he gathered her up into a warm embrace, his lips meeting hers. They tasted like mud and watermelon, an odd but stimulating flavor. Her arms found their place around his neck, and she kissed him harder, deeper than before.

Ty could feel natural emotion flowing through her kiss. She was feeling every ounce that he provided her. As a matter of a fact, she was eating it up as if she had been starved for years. Greed started to take over, and she became more intense; her tongue became more adventurous. Ty felt his balance falter, and before he could regain the upper hand, her greedy desire pushed both of them over and onto the mud-covered ground.

The thick pasty substance mashed around his back as she laid herself on top of him. Her lips never left his as her hands explored every inch of exposed skin.

Ty didn't know much about her BDSM relationship, but from what little Grace had told him he believed she had never been allowed to touch Ben at will. Her actions confirmed that as she ran her dirty hands over every cell along his belly as if she had never felt skin like his.

She left fire along the trails she traced, and it felt like she was playing connect the dots with each mud splatter.

Ty couldn't take it anymore. With her straddled across his waist, he sat up and pushed his hands into her hair and loosened the already loose ponytail.

"I want to get dirty," she cooed against his lips.

"Really?" he teased. "Then you'll need to remove your shirt so we can get you dirty."

Her tempting smile almost pushed him over the edge as she

grabbed the hem of her shirt and hoisted it over her head. She wore a pretty royal blue –and tan lace bra. It was almost a shame to ruin it.

"You sure you want to get this pretty thing dirty?" Ty asked her and brushed his hand along the lace of the bra.

She didn't answer; she just reached down and grabbed a handful of mud and smeared it across her chest and coated the expensive bra with the organic dirt.

Ty smiled and grabbed another handful of mud, playfully smearing it across her belly. She looked hot. Ty didn't know how much longer he could contain his libido.

"Come here," he told her, crushing her chest against his, and returning his mouth to hers.

She kissed his lips deeply and stung him with the intense passion she was feeling. He cupped her butt and rolled her onto the ground so the mud coated her back. Then he brought his fingers to the button of her jean shorts and released the hold they had on her hips.

He was surprised to find she wasn't wearing any underwear. Her nether regions were perfectly groomed and unaffected by the dirty mud that painted the rest of her skin.

His eyes met hers with a smile, and the invitation she returned set him into motion immediately.

He relieved himself of his jeans and sought the one place his body craved to be. She encased him with warmth, and it was the most heavenly place he could be at the moment. He began to thrust into her; his hips moved in a rhythm they had shared only one other time. She moaned in pleasure as he thrust deeper and deeper inside her as he sought release from the building pressure in his member. Her breathing increased with his, and they climbed together as his thrusts were met with a sway of her hips.

He sensed her imminent release as well, and he brought his lips to hers as they shuddered together in a combined release that neither one of them had ever experienced. It felt as though the stars had fallen around them that night, as if fireworks were sparkling and booming as they crashed together.

"Grace, I love you," he whispered against her sated lips.

He slowly removed himself from the warmth of her body and caressed her face.

"I love you too," she answered as her eyes held his and confirmed the truth.

EPILOGUE

$\mathcal{T}$y leaned back against his black truck, observing the finished park in front of him. Freshly painted buildings, which hadn't yet been used by the public, waited to be revealed later that day during the city's ribbon cutting ceremony. Today's job was to ensure everything was done, every item on the final punch list completed before the mayor and his group of city officials stepped foot on the premises.

Ty took a sip of coffee from the mug in his left hand, the hot liquid sliding down his throat at a refreshing pace. He noticed several things that needed attention right off the bat; a missed corner of the building soffit that hadn't been painted, several pieces of construction litter thrown in the grass to the left of the building, a light fixture outside the bathroom door missing a light bulb and two bushes that didn't survive their initial planting.

He'd have Alejandro handle those items when he arrived and he would trust they would get done while he was gone. He needed to be at another jobsite, going over the new scope of work and then he needed to shower and dress for the ribbon cutting. This was the first time he and Grace would introduce themselves as co-owners of Evans' Construction.

This was also the first time they'd share that they were getting married.

Married.

Alejandro pulled into the parking lot, his aged car sputtering before it rested in the final spot. Alejandro climbed out, slamming the door behind him to ensure it would hold itself in place. He approached Ty with a coffee mug in one hand and his cell phone in the other.

"Morning, Boss," he said as he slid his phone in his back pocket.

"Morning. I've gotta get over to Grand Hut. Your list is easy and short," Ty answered, handing him the written punch list.

"Got it. Do you want me to sign off on each item on this paper?"

"Yeah and give it to Karen when you're done. Then go to the Hughman's residence to help John."

"Okay."

Feeling satisfied, Ty nodded and climbed into his truck.

"Don't forget the soffit," he said as his truck roared to life. He rolled down the windows, allowing the cool spring breeze to fill the cab and waved to Alejandro one last time before pulling out into traffic.

Just as he turned up the radio to listen to his favorite song his phone rang over the Bluetooth connection. The screen on his dash read 'Grace Evans'.

"Good morning, Mrs. Parks." His voice held a hint of seduction and excitement at the same time.

"Not yet, but good morning. You at Riverwalk?"

He turned the volume button several clicks to the right so that Grace's voice was a little louder. "No, I just left. Why?"

"No reason. Just wondered if you were busy."

"Never too busy for you." He could almost sense her blush through the speakers.

"Are you ready for this afternoon?"

"What? To tell everyone that you agreed to marry me?" He couldn't help but smile.

"Yes, silly."

"Of course I am. Are you?"

"I'm a little nervous. I'm worried everyone will think I only agreed because of my dad's will."

"Well, isn't that why?" He teased.

"No." She drew out the word.

"Good."

"What are you wearing?" she asked.

"Right now?"

"No silly, to the ribbon cutting."

"Oh, jeans and a dress shirt. You?"

"I found a cute dress a couple of weeks ago."

"Oh, I can't wait to see it. Rather, see you in it," he hinted, taking a left hand turn onto the beachside road. He rode along with traffic, at a slow speed.

"Ty," she giggled and the light tension in her voice brought a smile to Ty's face.

Out of the corner of his eye he saw a flash of red in his passenger side mirror. It was sudden and it was in front of him before he could grasp where it came from. The driver, an impatient teenage boy probably rushing to get on the beach, darted in and out of several cars in front of him. Ty shifted his attention from Grace to the impatient driver.

The boy sped between two more cars and crossed in front of the one on the right, taking a sudden turn onto the beach ramp. He must not have seen the motorcycle in front of that car and before he could react, he collided with it. Several cars in front of Ty slammed on their brakes, their red lights drawing attention to the sudden halt the teenager's actions had created. Ty slammed on his brakes and that, as well as, the loud screech of the rubber tires sliding across the road made its way to Grace.

"What was that?"

"I've gotta go. A boy just hit a motorcycle with his car."

Ty hung up the line and climbed out. He focused on the motorcyclist lying on the ground, his bright yellow bike tossed on its side. The teenage boy wasn't getting out of his car and no one was taking action.

"You okay?" Ty asked when he reached the motorcyclist, placing his hand on his shoulder.

He didn't respond at first but started to move, curling himself in a fetal position. Pain. Ty knew that meant pain.

"Stay here. Don't move. I'm calling an ambulance." He rushed back to his truck and grabbed his phone from the center cup holder, dialing 911.

"911, what's your emergency."

"Yes, I'm on A1A in front of the Grand Hut. A motorcyclist has been hit. Please send an ambulance."

"Okay. Is it a man or woman?"

"Man. He's got a helmet on so I can't say much about his face."

"Is he breathing?"

"Yes. He's curled into a ball, so I assume it's internal to his abdomen."

"An officer is on his way. Please remain on the line with me."

"I will."

"Is the... off to... the road..." Dispatch was cut off as Grace tried to return his call.

Ty ignored her call and continued to talk, "I'm sorry. You cut out."

"Is the motorcycle off the road?"

"Yes."

"Has the rider been moved?"

"No. Like I said before, he is curled into a ball."

"Okay, that's a good sign. An officer should be there shortly."

At the sound of the sirens, Ty stepped closer to the edge of the road, his eyes landing on the teenager who never made an attempt to leave his car; either he was too startled or didn't care. Either way, he remained in his small, red Honda Civic while his victim moaned from the ground, cell phone plastered to his ear.

"Hey, I hope you're on the phone with your parents!" Ty yelled to him, pointing to the damage he had caused.

The boy turned his head and continued his conversation.

Ty finished the call with the dispatcher as an officer pulled up with his lights and sirens active.

"Sir, can you speak?" the officer asked the rider.

"I think my leg's broken and my chest hurts." The words were difficult for the man to speak. Paramedics pulled up next, clearing the scene and attending to the victim.

Ty watched as they unbuckled the man's full face helmet and lifted it from his head. Ty took a startled step backward, his breath getting caught in his throat.

"Ben?" It wasn't meant to be heard by anyone else but rather was a statement of surprise as he backed away from the scene and allowed the paramedics and police to do their jobs.

All sorts of emotions ran through Ty as he struggled to compose himself, bending at the knee to bring himself closer to the ground and steady himself with his hands.

A crowd was gathering now, as tourists and other motorists stopped to watch. A woman stepped up and offered a bottle of water to Ty, allowing him the opportunity to step back.

He turned back one last time to see Ben being lifted into the ambulance on a stretcher, his eyes fixed on Ty.

All Ty could think was: *Karma's a Bitch.*

The End

STELLA GRACE

Have you ever read a book that kept you turning pages until 2 a.m., only to be let down by the outcome? Stella Grace had that happen too many times and that's why she started writing. She has been writing since middle school. She is now married to her high school sweetheart and they share two children. She lives in sunny Florida but desires life in the Georgia mountains. She is a huge historical romance fan but hasn't yet written in that genre herself. She prefers modern romance stories with feisty women and dominant men. She is a restless soul who loves to travel and provide her kids with as many experiences as she can. She holds a degree in Psychology, which her husband hates because she actually understands him.

Find Stella on Facebook
Check out her website at: www.authorstellagrace.com

Don't miss these exciting titles by Stella Grace and Blushing Books!

Renovating His Heart

Made in the USA
Middletown, DE
10 August 2018